Love Song

Love Song

Adam Kennedy

The Viking Press · New York

First published in 1976 by The Viking Press
625 Madison Avenue, New York, N.Y. 10022

Published simultaneously in Canada by
The Macmillan Company of Canada Limited

LIBRARY OF CONGRESS CATALOGING IN PUBLICATION DATA
Kennedy, Adam.
Love song.
I. Title
PZ4.K343Lo [PS3561.E425]   813'.5'4   76–21052
ISBN 0–670–44298–4

Printed in the United States of America

For Anna Marie and Susan
  the best two women I know
and for Fred Bergmann
  my teacher and permanent friend

Feather beds are soft, and painted rooms are bonny.
I would trade them all for my handsome, winsome Johnny.

Some say he's black, but I say he's bonny.
Fairest of them all is my handsome, winsome Johnny.

I know where I'm going, and I know who's going with me.
I know who I love, but the dear knows who I'll marry.

—Scottish folk ballad

Part One

I

When innocence is laughable, when intelligence is suspect and destruction becomes a creative act, when pragmatism is the ultimate philosophy and greed the penultimate drive, when expedience rules . . . in such a time, each state and county and village becomes its own Dachau, primitive and secular, structured to serve local needs, fueled by local victims, names like Miller and Johnson, Solomon, Banasac, and Bernstein, Hoffman, and Bellini. They live in a cage of wrong values and die at last, scarred and bewildered by ideas they never understood. Flags across their coffins, Bibles in their hands, rouge and powder on their cheeks, they make mute exits from a world they neither enriched nor enjoyed. And their friends, leaving the graveside, go to their cars, drive to their homes, eat poisoned food, breathe poisoned air, shake their heads in confusion, and wait their turns.

Jossie Floyd was lucky. She knew none of this. She was twenty years old and full of tomorrow.

2

Climaxing a painful year, harbinger, perhaps, of a private doomsday, it was a critical day for her, every minute scheduled, every detail planned.

That afternoon, however, at two o'clock, Theron called. "I'm sorry, kid. I know you worked it out with Ethel for the three to eleven. But she just called in sick."

"She wasn't sick last night," Jossie said. "I saw her when she got off work. She was out to set a few world's records."

"Well, maybe she set some. Cause she's out of commission now."

"Did you see her?"

"No. I talked to her on the phone. Just hung up before I called you."

"Let me call her. I'll get her in there, I promise you."

"Good. I wish you luck. But if she can't hack it, you'll have to fill in. Otherwise I'll be sweating blood."

She hung up, then dialed Ethel. When she answered Jossie said, "What are you doing to me?"

"I knew it was you soon as I heard the phone ring. I said so to Dale."

"Dale? What's he doing there? Theron said you were sick."

"I am. Like a dog. I got a headache, a fever, and the trots. You name it, I've got it."

"Then what the hell is Dale doing there?"

"He's just leaving."

"I'll bet he is. Just leaving the bed to pour himself another drink."

"Come on, kid, give me a break. I promised you . . ."

"I know you did. That's what I'm talking about."

". . . but I just can't cut it. I'm really a mess. Theron

wouldn't let me work if I did go in."

"You want to bet on that? Why don't you try it and see?"

"I can't, honey. It's not my fault. I really can't."

"You knew how important it was for me to get off work today. I have to get myself ready to leave. I told you that a dozen times."

"I know you did. And I feel awful about it."

"I'll bet you do."

"It doesn't do any good to get snotty about it."

"Yes, it does," Jossie said. "It does *me* some good."

She hung up the phone, quickly put on her uniform, borrowed Mr. Massengale's car, and drove to work. It was almost midnight when she got home. She took a bath and washed her hair. Then she straightened up her room and packed a suitcase while she waited for her hair to dry. It was after two o'clock before she went to sleep.

At five the alarm woke her up. She got dressed quickly and had coffee downstairs in the kitchen with Mr. Massengale and his wife. Then he drove her into Pittsburgh to the main bus station.

"I hate to take you out of your way like this," she said.

"No skin off me. I'll get to clock in early, that's all. Beat the morning jam-up for a change."

When he pulled in at the curb by the bus station, he said, "You enjoy yourself now. And drop us a card if you get a minute. Though I figure you'll be too taken up for that. Too busy lollygagging that corporal."

"I wouldn't be surprised."

"How long is it you'll be gone? Ruby couldn't get it straight."

"Ten days, two weeks, I guess. It's all according to how much time Kermit has off. I told Theron to expect me when he sees me."

"Well, we'll be thinking about you. And don't worry about things here. Me and Ruby'll hold the fort."

Inside the terminal, at the ticket window, she said, "You got a bus to Huntington at seven o'clock?"

"That's correct." The agent was a thin black man with a scar-welt across his nose, a brown cigarette at the corner of his mouth.

"I need a ticket to Weston."

"Round-trip?"

"I don't know. Do I save any money that way?"

The agent shook his head and smoke trailed out through his nostrils. "Coming back costs the same as going."

"Then I'll just take the one-way. That way I won't have to worry about losing half of my ticket. Or if it turns out I'm not coming back I won't have to cash it in."

"Makes sense to me," the ticket agent said.

At the departure gate, a shifting cluster of people tailed away to a ragged line, parcels and satchels scattered around them, cartons tied with twine, a stale popcorn smell in the air, the floor stained and sticky from dripping ice cream and spilled soft drinks.

As Jossie set her bag down, a man wearing a green jacket with metal buttons, a heavy tan suitcase in his hand, got in line just behind her. "I'm looking for the Huntington bus and they pointed me this way. Is this the right line?"

"It better be," Jossie said. "I'm counting on it."

He set his bag down, buttoned his jacket, and smoothed his hair back with one hand. "I'm not what you'd call a steady bus-rider. I mean I'm not exactly a *regular.*" He fished a pack of cigarettes out of his shirt pocket.

"Can I offer you a Tareyton filter-tip?"

Jossie looked at him for the first time. Sideburns down to his jaw line, tinted glasses, and a strong, sweet scent, cologne mixed with perspiration and last night's bourbon, misting off his body. "No, thanks," she said. "I don't smoke."

He lit his cigarette, eased himself around to where he could see her face, and went on talking. "The thing that happened was my Pontiac broke down. Brand new car, practically . . . a Star-bird, full power, bucket seats. The company gets me a new one every year about this time. A nice color, too. Sort of a maroon I guess you'd call it, red vinyl seats and carpet to match. Only two or three thousand miles on her, not even broken in good, still got that showroom smell. But last night when I pulled into the garage at the motor inn, she just coughed and died on me. I'm pretty handy with tools, a good man with motors and the like, but I couldn't even make her sputter. I got a young fella from the Gulf station across the street to come over and he had his head under the hood for half an hour. But he couldn't do any better than I did. So . . . that's it. My wheels are in the Pontiac garage getting operated on and I'm flogging my way to Charleston on some go-to-hell bus." He took a deep survival drag on his cigarette and said, "Are you a resident of Pittsburgh?" He moved another half-step around and stood with his back to the departure gate. She looked up at him slowly, fixed him with her eyes like a moth on a pin, and said nothing.

"I mean do you live here in Pittsburgh or . . ."

"I heard what you said. It's none of your business."

"Hey, now. It's too early in the morning. No need to get huffy."

"I'm not huffy. I just said it's none of your God-damned business where I live."

Two gray-haired women, ahead of Jossie in the line, turned around so they could hear better. The man noticed them and his voice was quieter when he answered, talking through a pasted-on smile.

"Now, wait a minute . . . there's no reason to smart off to me, honey. I was just trying to be friendly."

"No, you weren't," Jossie said. "You're trying for *something* all right but *friendly* is not the word for it. You know it and *I* know it."

The gray-haired women giggled and the man's voice dropped even lower. "Listen to me, you little split-tail."

"No, you listen to *me*. Where I work I see fifty guys a day like you. Same clothes, same perfume, the same sad line of bullshit. It's hard enough to listen when I'm getting paid. But now I'm on my own time and I don't want to listen at all. Is that plain enough for you?"

A voice from the front of the line floated back. "She's gettin' him straightened out, ain't she?" Another voice said, "Let him have it, dew-drop!" and several people laughed.

The man squared himself solid, puffed on his cigarette, and his voice ground down to a whisper. "Where the hell you get off talking to me like that? Little eighteen-year-old slut."

"Twenty," Jossie said.

"Twitching your ass around so somebody might look at you, then getting on your high horse if anybody does."

Something in her eyes stopped him. "Just keep it up," she said. "You keep mouthing off like that and I'll give you a shot right where your money is. One more word out of you is all I need. I'll kick you so hard you'll have to sit down to pee."

"Whoooeee!" Another voice from up front.

The man in the green jacket stood like a totem. Finally he broke. "God-damned bus station. Nothing but hookers and hay-shakers." He reached down, picked up his bag and swaggered across the terminal to the coffee machine. When they called the Huntington bus he was the last one to get on. He blustered back through the aisle, grumbling to himself, eyes straight ahead, and took a seat in the last row.

One of the gray-haired women looked across the aisle at Jossie and said, "I don't think that gentleman *likes* us."

"No, I guess not," Jossie said.

3

It was eight minutes past seven when the bus crawled out of the terminal, moved southwest through the geometric tangle of Pittsburgh, and on through the suburbs to pick up Interstate 79. At seven forty-five they stopped at the downtown terminal in Washington, Pennsylvania. At eight thirty they rolled through Waynesburg, and twenty-three minutes later they crossed the state line into West Virginia, stopping in Morgantown at sixteen minutes past nine. On south then, through Fairmount and Stonewood, arriving in Weston at last at eleven fourteen, Jossie dead-tired all the way, her forehead hot, her eyes burning, but too excited to sleep.

As she stepped down from the bus she saw Chet wheel in on Kermit's motorcycle, the paint scratched and scarred, rust on the rims, the sidecar swaying and bumping, tires whining on the asphalt. He swung off the saddle and walked across the driveway to meet her.

"Hey, burr-head, you're late. This is my second trip over here from the tavern." He put his arms around her and kissed her on the cheek. "Just like old times."

"Jesus, what happened to you?" she said.

He picked up her bag and they walked between two lines of parked cars toward the motorcycle. "You mean what's been happening right along or the last couple of days or what?"

"I mean you look like you've been hanging upside down. For a month or so."

Still walking, one arm around her shoulders, he leaned over and kissed her again. "You know why I can't get along without you? I miss all that abuse. Every place I go women fall all over me. They can't seem to do enough for me. And all the time I keep thinking, 'Where in the hell is Jossie? There's a girl that knows how to make a man *bleed.*' It's the truth. I miss it. If I ever had a sister I'd want her to be just like you. Mean and ugly."

"Never mind the crap," she said. "Are you hung over or what?"

"I'm a little hung over and a lot hungry and I've only got thirty-seven cents. How about you?"

"I'm starving to death and I've got some money."

They went to a restaurant on the town square, half a block cater-corner from the bus station. They sat in a booth by the window so Chet could watch the motorcycle at the curb, Jossie's suitcase lashed across the tail-end of the sidecar.

"Well," he said. "You really grew up, didn't you?"

"I haven't changed so much."

"You don't think so, huh? Why do you think those limber-dicks at the counter are falling off their stools trying to get a good look at you?"

"I didn't notice."

"Last time I saw you I had a bigger chest than you did . . ."

"Not the way I remember it."

". . . now you look like you're smuggling grapefruit out of the A & P store."

"You're crazy. I still wear the same size brassiere I wore when I was fifteen."

"Jesus. Is it that long since I saw you?"

"Not quite. But it's four years. Since right before Kermit enlisted and you went off with your shirt-tail out to whip the world. Judging from the way you look, I'd say the world got in a few more licks than *you* did."

"There you go again," he said.

"Well, it's the truth."

"No, it ain't. I won a few and lost a few maybe. But I didn't go under. I mean I've been wet a few times but I haven't drowned yet."

"Agnes wrote me you've been getting around the country some."

"Yeah, I guess so."

"She says you've covered the whole map pretty near."

"Well, I didn't go to Vermont yet. Nor the Dakotas. But every other state I took a taste of at least once. And some of them, like California and New York and Florida, I've been in and out of quite a bit."

"How long you been back here in Kittredge?"

"Six or seven weeks, I guess. I got here in June, right after they buried Kermit's mother. Three or four days later, they told me it was."

"I must have just missed you."

"That's what Agnes said. She told me you came down for the funeral."

Jossie nodded her head. "I felt like I had to. Kermit's mother was closer to me in a lot of ways than my own folks. Same thing with you. Mrs. Docker couldn't have treated you any better if you'd been Kermit's own brother. Remember when she used to open the kitchen door and holler out, 'How many kids have I got for supper?' Most days it was four. Her own two and you and me, squeezed right up to the table with Kermit and Agnes."

"Seems like a couple hundred years ago."

After they finished eating, Jossie said, "Where you staying while you're here?"

"Up at the Docker place. Nobody there since the funeral so Agnes said I might as well. Helps keep the coons and the groundhogs out."

"I'm surprised Agnes and Melvin didn't move in there."

"They talked about it, I guess. But you know Melvin. He hates to budge too far from his gas pumps. He'd shoot himself, sure as hell, if he ever missed out on a customer. This way, living next door to the garage, he figures he's open for business twenty-four hours a day. Somebody honks their horn at three in the morning, he's right out there in his underwear wiping off the windshield and checking the oil."

"Melvin's crazy. He's a hog for money."

"Agnes says as much time as he spends working she's surprised they ever had any kids at all."

"She's doing pretty good," Jossie said. "Twenty-five years old and she's got six already."

"That's what I told her. I said it's a good thing for her that Melvin's working all the time. Otherwise she might have a dozen kids."

"What did she say?"

"She just laughed. You know how Agnes is."

The waitress brought the check and Jossie paid it.

"Thanks for the food," Chet said. "That's two pork chops and a plate of beans I owe you."

"I'll give you my address," she said, "and you can send me a check." She opened her purse and put the change inside. "You think Kermit's going to bunk up there with you?"

"He'd better. We've got a lot to talk about. Besides, Agnes doesn't have much extra room. There's a kid in every corner."

"Well, in that case, I guess I'll stay up there, too."

"Suit yourself," Chet said.

"What's that supposed to mean? Are you saying you'd

like it better if I stayed someplace else?"

"No, I didn't say that. I just meant . . ."

"What?"

"Nothing."

"Come on, Chet. Spit it out."

"Well, I was just thinking about Kermit."

"What about him?

"That's what I don't know. I mean things aren't exactly like they used to be."

"They are as far as I'm concerned," Jossie said.

"Maybe so. But what about him?"

"Did he say something to you? Did he write anything about me?"

"He didn't have to. I can figure out a few things for myself."

"Like what?"

"Oh, for Christ's sake, Jossie. Stop kidding yourself. You can't pretend nothing happened."

"I'm not trying to pretend anything. I don't have to. Kermit knows what I did and why I did it. I explained it all to him. I've been writing to him over there in Germany for the last six months or so."

"Yeah, I know. Agnes told me."

They got up and walked out of the restaurant into the sunshine. "I wrote him just two weeks ago," Jossie said. "Four pages. Air mail."

They crossed the sidewalk and she climbed into the sidecar. Chet swung on from the other side and settled himself in the saddle. "The other thing Agnes told me is you haven't had answers to those letters."

"So what? I don't care what Agnes says. I don't care what anybody says. I don't need a lot of people sticking their nose in."

"I'm not sticking my nose in. I just don't want you to count on something . . . I mean, I don't want you to get your feelings hurt."

"Don't worry about my feelings. I'll worry about that. I've had a lot of time to think. I know what I want to do and I'm going to do it. You don't have to be on my side if you don't want to. I'm not asking you for any help. But I don't need anybody to screw me up either."

He tramped on the starter pedal and the cycle engine roared. He idled it down and leaned close to Jossie, laughing. "I was wrong about you. You haven't changed a bit."

4

They headed east on Highway 33, through Horner and Lorentz to Buckhannon, then on east to Elkins, south from there on 219 to Beverly, then due east on a badly kept tarvy road into the mountains, toward Kittredge.

Just before they came to the edge of town, Chet shouted, "All right with you if we go the back way?" Jossie nodded her head and he angled off on a rutted road, powdery dust in the hollows, tufted grass on the center hump, weeds and vines tangling together on the narrow roadside shoulders.

The road twisted and climbed. At last Chet turned off again, up a steep lane, rail-fenced on either side. They bumped and skidded and bounced thirty or forty yards up the lane and slid to a stop at last in a grassy clearing, walled in on all sides by thick stands of spruce and evergreen, walnut, hickory, and yellow poplar. Patches of azalea, aster, rhododendron, and laurel sprawled everywhere. Morning glories, blue and purple, tangled their vines around the tree trunks. And an angular, gray and weathered frame house stood in one corner of the clearing.

After Jossie had climbed out of the sidecar, Chet

wheeled the cycle into a patch of shade by the house and unstrapped her suitcase.

"I can't believe it's the same place," she said. She stood near the porch, looking out toward the cow barn and the hog sheds and the chicken house, rough and unpainted, starting to lean, shingles missing, weeds on the paths, the outhouse door sagging open, the wire fence trampled down around the burial plot, burdock and thistle overgrowing the headstones. "Only a few weeks since the funeral and already it's going to seed."

She stepped up on the porch and went into the house, Chet, with her bag, trailing behind her.

"Jesus, Chet. What have you been doing in here?"

"Sleeping and eating. What's the matter?"

"Did you ever open a window?"

"I tried it. But too much dirt blew in."

"I'm talking about some dirt blowing *out.*"

"I never claimed to be a housekeeper," he said.

"You never claimed to be a hog either. But you've sure been living like one."

"Don't worry about it. It suits me all right."

"Well, it doesn't suit *me.* And it won't suit Kermit."

"Why not? He's lived here most of his life."

"Not like this." She looked at her watch. "I've got to get busy. It's getting on to two o'clock. What time's he due in?"

"Four twenty in Elkins. Four thirty-five at the Beverly junction."

"Well, two hours is better than nothing." She picked up her suitcase, carried it to the kitchen table, and opened it. Then she unzipped her dress in the back and pulled it off over her head. She folded it and hung it across a chair back. When she looked around Chet was staring at her. "What are you gawking at?"

"I'm gawking at *you,*" he said. "Who wouldn't?"

"Oh, come on, Chet, cut out the crap. You've seen

girls in their underwear before. It's a cinch you've seen *me*. We've been swimming bare since we were six years old. Now all of a sudden you're staring at me like I grew an extra boob or something. It's the same old carcass. No better, no worse. I've still got a crooked toe on my left foot and you've got a birthmark on your behind shaped like an arrowhead. The left cheek. Right?"

He began to laugh and she said, "Unless maybe you had it sliced off by some society doctor." She pulled a pair of jeans out of the bag and started to put them on.

"Nope. It's still there."

"That's good. I'd hate to bump into you at a nudist camp and not be able to recognize you."

For two hours Chet pulled weeds and swung a sickle in the yard, propped up fences, and tightened hinges while Jossie swept and dusted and scrubbed the inside of the house. The parlor, the kitchen, the downstairs bedroom, and the sleeping loft at the top of the ladder.

At three forty-five she went out on the porch and called to Chet. "You'd better get going. By the time you wash up, change your shirt, and get into Elkins, he ought to be there."

"Who said anything about me changing my shirt?"

"*I* did. You smell like a raccoon."

"I wasn't planning to go all the way into Elkins either. I figure the driver'll let him get out at the Beverly turn-off."

"Oh, for Pete's sake, Chet, put yourself out a little. He's coming all the way from Germany. Can't you drag your tail a few extra miles into Elkins?"

Chet stripped off his shirt and washed himself in a pan on the well platform. He put on a clean shirt, then slicked his hair back with water, poured three fingers of bourbon into a jelly glass and drank it. "Here I go," he said. "How do I look?"

"Like a blue-ribbon boar. I'm proud of you." She walked out to the motorcycle with him. "Do me a favor. Don't tell Kermit I'm here. I want to surprise him."

"You think that's a good idea?"

"Never mind if it's a good idea or not. I just asked you to do me a favor. If you don't want to, I can't force you. I can't . . ."

"Hey, what are you crying about? Jesus . . . all smiles one minute and then you're crying like a baby. Look, I'm sorry. I didn't mean to . . ."

She turned and ran into the house. Chet followed her and found her in a corner of the bedroom, her shoulders shaking, her forehead pressed against the wall.

"Come on now. Cut it out. I won't tell him you're here."

He turned her around slowly till her head rested against his chest.

"You keep bawling like that, you're gonna look like hell." He put his arms around her and said, "Jesus, I wish you'd stop it. What's the matter? Tell me what's wrong."

She pushed away from him suddenly. "What's wrong? God, you're dumb. I'm scared to death. That's what's wrong."

"You're not scared of Kermit, are you?"

"I'm not scared *of* him. I'm just scared to *see* him. I'm scared of what he's liable to say. I keep telling myself I'll pump out a tub full of water and take a nice bath, put some perfume on and a pretty dress. Then he'll come walking through the door and everything will be like it used to be."

"I didn't say it *wouldn't* be that way," Chet said.

"Maybe not. But that's what you meant. And maybe you're right. He might take one look at me and say . . . I don't know what he's liable to say, but whatever it is, it scares me."

"First time I ever saw you scared of anything."

"Well, take a good look so you'll remember what it was like."

"It wouldn't surprise me if he's as anxious to see you as you are to see him.

"Then why didn't he answer my letters?"

"I can't answer that."

"I can't either. That's what scares me."

5

Five people got off the bus in Elkins, a gaunt, sunburned man in bib overalls, a pregnant woman in a cotton dress, and two small children, one clutching a quart bottle of cola, the other one with a pacifier in his mouth. Last off was Kermit, trim and hard and hatless, brown hair cut short, carrying his duffel roll on a long strap, a small canvas bag in his other hand.

"You son-of-a-bitch," he said when he saw Chet. "Agnes wrote me you'd be here but I told her I wouldn't believe it till it happened."

"You're looking good," Chet said.

"You, too."

"No, I'm not. And I know it. I look like I been through the wringer."

"What's the matter?"

"Off my feed a little. That's all. Nothing a stiff drink won't fix."

"Good. Let's get one." He looked off across the street. "I see Beaudine's is still there."

"That's right. Same old rat hole."

They walked away from the bus station toward the tavern. "You'll have to treat this time," Chet said. "I'm a little short."

"You're always a little short."

"Don't worry. I'll pay you back."

"No, you won't. Long as I'm here, I'm popping. Your money won't buy shit."

They sat in the late afternoon cool of the tavern, pool balls clicking in the back room, cards slapping down on a table in the corner, voices on the juke box complaining softly about desertion and adultery.

"Four years?"

"Right at it," Chet said.

"And you've been all over everywhere, I hear."

"Not like you. I haven't been out of the country."

"Sure you have. What about that card you sent me from Tijuana? A naked girl straddling a jackass."

"That's right. I forgot about that. I ended up with the clap down there."

"What kind of news is that? You used to get the clap more times than you got a haircut."

"Not now. Now I get more haircuts. I'm hanging out with a better crowd."

"Sounds that way. Palm Beach, Agnes said. You still down there?"

"That's still my mailing address. I mean that's where I was till I came up here a few weeks ago."

"What about your wife?" Kermit said.

"That's a good question. What about her?"

"You still married or not?"

"In a way I am and in a way I'm not."

"You mean you're only married when you're home?"

"Something like that. It's a long story. I'll tell you all about it sometime when I'm drunk. It sounds better then." He pointed to the chevrons on Kermit's sleeve. "I see you got *two* of those doo-dads. That means you're a corporal. Right?"

"That's it. I'm gradually taking over the whole works. And we just got our pay jacked up. Four hundred and thirty a month."

"You're lucky you don't have to live on that here. In Palm Beach they charge you a dollar to take a crap. And that's just the base price. You have to bring your own paper."

"Are you working down there or what?"

"Well . . . I *used* to work. I was tending bar in one of the hotels till I got married. Now I just work my peter mostly and live off Sarah."

"Is that your wife's name?"

"That's one of them. She's got more names than a phone book. Those society women have a lot of names. And they add another one every time they get married. By the time they're forty it sounds like the Pittsburgh Steelers lineup every time they get introduced."

"You got a picture of her?" Kermit said. "I'd like to see what she looks like."

"No, you wouldn't. Sarah never looked too good at her best. And the best was some time back."

"How old is she?"

"Don't ask me. I don't know and I don't *want* to know."

"I mean is she over thirty?"

"Over thirty? Don't make me laugh."

"Forty?"

"She was over forty when you and I were balancing on a milking stool trying to screw your Dad's Jersey heifer."

Kermit started to chuckle. "You bastard. You couldn't tell the truth if your life depended on it."

"I'm telling you . . . I never wore dark glasses till I met Sarah. For two weeks after we got married I had a doctor put drops in my eyes just to blur my vision. And every night before we go to bed I unplug all the lamps so there's no way she can switch one on when I'm humping her."

"Lying like a rug."

"I'm not lying. I wish I was."

"I know you. You screwed every good-looking girl in Randolph County. You're not about to end up with a dog."

"Don't take my word for it. Whenever you've got some time on your hands, just drop in to Palm Beach and see for yourself. Nothing I say about her could be half as bad as looking at the real thing."

"Then why'd you marry her?"

"That's another good question." Chet emptied his glass. "Let's have a drink on that."

Kermit held up two fingers and said to the bartender, "Give us a couple more, Harold." He turned back to Chet.

"I'm still waiting. Why'd you marry her?"

"I figured it beat working."

"Just like that?"

"That's it. I was tired of bumming around the country. Breaking my balls, mixing drinks, and taking shit from a lot of strangers. So when Sarah showed up one night, rolling her eyes and resting her tits on the bar like a pillow, I thought, 'What the hell. I got nothing to lose. I'll be a male whore for a while.'"

"You mean she's got some money?"

"Money? She's got so much money she don't even need money. Take a fine-tooth comb to her house and you wouldn't find a dime. I mean it. She just signs her name. Every place she goes. Restaurants, gas stations, department stores. All she needs is a pen. That's where she's got me. As long as I'm with her, I can buy any fucking thing I want. I mean she'll sign her name to anything. But when I'm by myself. Zero. I can't afford to use a pay toilet. I had to hock some of her clothes to get the bus fare up here. Took off one day while she was having her sinus passages blown out."

"Now what?"

"I don't know. I guess I'll hang around here till your

furlough is over. Then I'll call her collect and tell her to send me a plane ticket."

"If you don't like it there, why you going back?"

"Why not? As long as my pecker holds out it's as good a job as any. Palm Beach is full of guys like me living off pussy. There's no secret about it. Those women dress us all up and lead us around like show dogs. All a guy needs is his own teeth and a healthy cock and he can live like a prince. Matter of fact, the cock doesn't need to be that healthy either. A lot of those old hens would rather *talk* about it than *do* it."

"Does that include Sarah?"

"Oh, no. Not her. She's been stretched and scraped, plucked and tweezered and shaved. Eyes fixed, nose job, freckles bleached, and moles removed. And none of it did any good. She still looks like Yogi Berra. But in the koozie department it's another story. She's got a twat like a sausage grinder. Say hello to her and she's out of her clothes, flat on her back, and snapping her fingers. I pity the poor undertaker that has to embalm her. She's liable to get him by the tool and rigor mortis him to death."

6

It was still light, late afternoon, when the motorcycle popped and sputtered up the hill and stopped by the frame house in the clearing. Kermit untangled himself from the sidecar, looked slowly around the property, then walked across the barnyard, past the sheds, and up an easy incline to the burial plot.

Chet picked up the duffel bag and the canvas satchel and carried them into the house. He looked for Jossie in all the rooms but she wasn't there. He climbed the ladder to the sleeping loft. It was clean and scrubbed, the bed made, the windows open, the curtains blowing, but she wasn't there either. And her suitcase was nowhere in the house.

When he came outside again, Chet walked across to where Kermit was, standing on the knoll, looking down at the graves, at the rough board marker with his mother's name burned on it, at the brown and withered floral pieces held down by stakes and stones on the mound of dirt.

"Agnes said they were waiting for you to come home before they decided on a tombstone of some kind."

"Yeah, I know," Kermit said. "That's what she wrote me." He walked to the rear of the burial ground, then came back. "I've never been able to figure why they put dead people in the ground."

"Got to put them somewhere. Can't leave them sitting around the kitchen."

"You know what I mean."

"The Indians used to put them up in trees."

"That makes more sense than digging a hole and dumping somebody in it."

"In the cities they cremate a lot of people."

"Yeah. But that doesn't set right with me either."

"I never figured it mattered much what you did with the leftovers once the person inside the carcass is dead. It's like a shotgun shell. Once it's fired the empty casing isn't worth a whole hell of a lot. The truth is, when you're dead, you're dead."

"I guess so. But a lot of people have trouble dealing with that."

"Sure they do. Because they're all screwed up by the Bible. You stick too close to what it says in the Bible and it's a one-way trip to the nut house."

"You never could have told Mom that. To her the gospel was the gospel."

"My folks too. Hellfire for breakfast and damnation for supper. They figure it's all right to have a horseshit life as long as you die happy. Not me. I can't swallow it."

They turned and walked toward the house. Kermit studied the barns and sheds, the pens and fences. "Sure looks run-down."

"I tried to fix things up a little," Chet said.

"I mean it always was run-down. I just never noticed it so much before. I look at this place now and I wonder how it ever supported us. I don't see how my folks managed to scratch out any kind of a living at all."

On the porch, Kermit turned and looked back across the clearing, losing color now in the afternoon light. "When you think about it," he said, "nobody in this county ever had an easy day. Nothing ever came smooth and tasting good. But now it's worse than ever. We're timbered out and farmed out and the coal's gone. Or else they tell you it costs too much to dig it out of the ground. None of it makes any sense. Families breaking up, leaving their houses to rot while they go off somewhere to scratch for a living. It's all shit."

As they turned toward the door, Chet said, "The only answer I know is to booze a little and screw a lot."

Inside the house, Kermit said, "Hey, you really did yourself a job in here. Clean as a whistle. The place even smells good. What did you do, take to wearing perfume?"

"Must be some new kind of detergent you smell. Or shaving lotion maybe."

Kermit wandered through the house, inspecting it, touching the furniture. Then he climbed the ladder to the loft. When he came down he said, "Bed all made up. Clean sheets. Just like a hotel. You're gonna make somebody a hell of a wife, Chet."

"Up yours, dog-face."

Chet reached a bottle of bourbon down from the cabinet shelf and they pulled up chairs to the kitchen table.

They sat there drinking and talking till the sun dropped to the rim of the west ridge and burned red through the window. Kermit stood up then, pumped some cistern water into his glass, emptied it, and turned it upside down on the drainboard.

"I'd better go down to see Agnes," he said. "She'll think it's funny if I put it off till tomorrow."

"I'll run you down there."

"You don't have to. I can walk it."

"Suit yourself. But I'm going anyway. Have a couple beers at Jernegan's and help out a little while Dude eats his supper."

"I'd better wise him up. With you behind the bar he could go broke in a hurry."

"Dead wrong. Never drink when I'm working."

"And never work when you're . . ."

"That's right."

In a tight thicket thirty yards from the house, Jossie stood watching, a carpet of moss under her feet, ferns thick around her legs, as Kermit and Chet came out of the house, laughing and talking, revved up the motorbike, and headed off down the hill road.

She waited till the engine sound softened and faded out. Then she walked slowly toward the house, burrs clinging to her dress, mud on her slippers, a smudge of dirt on one cheek and a thorn scratch on her forehead, carrying her suitcase first in one hand, then in the other.

Inside the house she struck a match and lighted a lamp. Then she stood immobile in the center of the floor. "God-damn it, anyway." She sat down on a chair by the kitchen table. "Son-of-a-bitching men."

Chet had left his glass on the table. She unscrewed the cap on the bourbon bottle and poured herself a drink. Elbows resting on the table, she drank it down steadily, a gulp at a time. Then she filled the glass again.

7

Kittredge was the first permanent settlement west of the Alleghenies, in the territory that would later become West Virginia. Jacob Kittredge, his wife and five children, and two other families, came there in 1753. They built cabins, cleared plots of ground, and planted vegetables. In the fall, however, a wandering band of Senecas attacked their compound, killing and burning. Only David Tygarts, an eleven-year-old boy, managed to escape.

Twelve years later, with his wife and two children and half a dozen stubborn timbermen and their families, Tygarts came back. Since that time, April 1765, there has been a continuing settlement called Kittredge, twenty-one people to begin with, over three thousand in 1911 when the lumber mills were operating full force, and four hundred and sixty-three now.

Shavers Fork still runs through the village, a brown trickle since 1952 because of the dam at Sizemore. And the railroad tracks are there. But they're rusted now, overgrown with grass and weeds, and never used.

The Kittredge residents, who shot deer and bear and grouse, grew potatoes, loomed wool, and tanned leather, are nurtured today by food stamps, welfare checks, and memories of another time.

Travelers who straggle in looking for gasoline, a public toilet, or something to eat are never instructed about the number of board-feet Kittredge once produced in a single month, the tons of soft coal. Eighteenth-century homes are not pointed out, frame sidings over log cores, deep windows proving the thickness of the walls.

And General Bob Garnett is never mentioned, hero in a losing cause at the nearby battle of Rich Mountain, July

11, 1861, commander of the rebel troops who were routed by McClellan's army and driven east across the mountains clear out of the state of West Virginia, leaving it to the federal troops.

These are the highlights of Kittredge history. But no one who lives there ever brings them up. Even among the oldest people, there is no sense of community. No one is proud to be there. Kittredge is a survival town, a leftover, nothing more.

8

Chet angled the motorcycle down the final slope onto the dusty main street, the motor grumbling and whining as he eased it along, barely enough light now to see the houses set back from the street on either side, lines of elm and oak in front, dandelions, black-eyed Susans, goldenrod, and sunflowers growing volunteer along the street. Daisies, petunias, asters, pansies, and dahlias in patches. And thick, strung-out clumps behind unpainted fences in the ill-kept yards, every rough and balding lawn studded with skeleton car frames, motors sitting up on stumps, bodies rusted and gutted, seats ripped out. And tires everywhere. Black rubber quoits leaning against trees, hanging from ropes, stacked in awkward tiers on front porches.

"A great place to buy a house and settle down," Kermit said.

"Yeah, it sure is. If you're a hundred and eight years old and half-dead from hoof-and-mouth disease."

He pulled up in front of a Mobil station dead-center in town, a single pump just at the edge of the road with a light burning over it and brighter lights in the garage twenty feet back, its doors open, a car up on jacks.

"Melvin must be getting ready for supper," Chet said. "Otherwise he'd be out here by now, hustling gas and kicking my tires."

"If I know Agnes, she's made him wash up a little because company's coming." He climbed out of the side-car. "I don't know why I'm riding in the sidecar. It's *my* motorcycle."

"Right you are. Just giving a little chauffeur service. We don't get many corporals around here."

"You coming in?" Kermit asked.

"No. You go ahead. I promised I'd give Dude a breather. When you're ready to go home, come on over and get me."

"It may be a little while. You know how Agnes is when she gets wound up."

"Don't worry about it. I'm not due anyplace."

9

Agnes Docker Culp, sister to Kermit, wife to Melvin, looking ten or fifteen years past her twenty-five, over-weight, out of shape, angry veins in her bare legs, her feet puffing out of carpet slippers, hair cut crude and short like a man's, sat at the round kitchen table, smoking a cigarette, the remains of dinner still on the plates and dishes, a five-month-old baby asleep against her shoulder.

"It was such a worry to me, Kermit. I didn't know what I ought to do. Melvin's not much use unless it's some-thing you can fix with a socket wrench. And when I finally got in touch with Dad down in Bluefield he was no help either. He kept blubbering on the phone and saying he'd be right along up here on the first bus he could catch. But, like I say . . ."

She ground out her cigarette on her plate and lit a

fresh one. "Finally, I thought about going to the Red Cross. Fact is, I didn't think of it, Mr. Armbruster, who's partners with the undertaker up in Elkins, put the notion in my head. He said, 'Get right on the phone to the Red Cross. They'll help you get word to Kermit. That's what they're good at.' So I went over to Jernegan's and Dude made the call for me, long distance. Closest office was up in Weston. He gave them all the particulars about where you were stationed and Mom dying and all, and sure enough they got the job done. But by the time they'd finally scared you up, Mom had been in the ground for three days."

She got up and walked to the open doorway of an adjoining room. The sounds of scuffling and outrage had begun to drown out the television set.

"Dwight Harold, this is the last time Mother's going to tell you. I'm having a grown-up talk here with your Uncle Kermit and I don't want to be jumping up and down every whipstitch. Either you hold yourself steady and keep an eye on brother and sister or you'll all march straight up to bed."

A small voice wailed something unintelligible, but his mother went on. "I won't have it now. And your dad won't have it either. Do you want him to take a strap to you?"

The room became silent suddenly. "That's what I thought. He'll be back inside here in a little bit and I don't want to have to give a bad report on you all." She started away, then turned back. "If you behave yourselves, I'll give you some cold R.C. and a Snickers bar before you go to bed."

She came back to the table and sat down. "They don't act that crazy as a rule. I expect they're excited because you're here." She took a sip of cold coffee. "What was I saying before?"

"About the Red Cross," Kermit said.

"Well, as it turned out it was just a waste. We only went to all that bother because we were in hopes of getting you back in time for the burial."

"If I'd been at my regular post in Hansa, I guess I could have made it. But like I told Melvin we were on maneuvers over by the Czech border. They had us sealed off tighter than a wad from everything and everybody."

"Just seems like a hell of a note."

"Yeah, I guess so."

"Finally, we couldn't wait any longer. But I felt awful about it. Dad away and you away . . ."

"I thought you said Dad came up as soon as you called him."

"He did. He was here all right. But for all the good he was, he might as well have stayed in Bluefield. You wouldn't *know* your dad the way he's changed. It's like somebody pulled the spine and bones right out of him. Oh, he looks all right. It's not that. His hair's pretty shaggy but he keeps himself clean. At least he did while he was here. And he had a decent suit of clothes for the services. But he's like a car without a battery. Can't get an answer out of him about anything. I don't even know where he's working. Or *if* he's working. Three years since he left Kittredge, right at it, and nobody knows anything about him since the day he left. Mom didn't know much. That's for sure. He used to scratch out a postcard to her every month or so, but that was it. One day he was here, strutting around and bragging to people the way he'd always done, and the next thing anybody knew he was long gone. Off to Bluefield."

Later, after she'd washed the dishes and put the children to bed, she said, "Come on, I'll walk you down to Jernegan's. I like to get a little air before I go to sleep. If I open the bedroom window, all I smell is gasoline."

They stopped downstairs in the garage so Kermit

could say good night to Melvin. Then they walked down the dark street toward the grocery store.

"Does the place seem different to you?" Agnes said.

"Not much."

"I don't think so either. Melvin says the whole county's changing, but I don't see it." Then she said, "What's happening with you and Jossie?"

"I don't know what to tell you."

"She's been writing to you, hasn't she?"

"Yeah, I had some letters from her."

"But she didn't get any back."

"Well, I'm not much of a hand to write."

"Melvin says he figures you've got a girl friend over there in Germany."

"Melvin figures everybody's got a girl friend everyplace."

"Have you?"

"Nobody special." He put his arm around his sister's waist and said, "You ought to write one of those newspaper columns telling people what to do about their love lives."

"Never mind that. I know you and Jossie had your ups and downs. But you're not likely to find anybody better. Just because she did a silly thing last year."

"Well, that's all over now," Kermit said.

"What does that mean?"

"Just what I said."

"Well, I don't like the sound of it. It's not manlike to go on whipping a person for something they did. Specially after they said they're sorry."

"I'm not whipping anybody."

"I don't know what you'd call it then. You don't answer any of her letters and now you say it's all over between you two. If that's the way you feel about it, the least you can do is tell her that to her face."

"Give me a break, Agnes. I don't want to talk about it any more."

"Maybe you don't. But *I* do."

10

Kermit sat at the counter in Jernegan's grocery store with an empty beer bottle in front of him.

"Have another one," Chet said.

"I don't think so. I'm gonna sack in."

"It ain't even ten o'clock yet."

"Depends on where you are. My system's still on German time. And it's four in the morning over there."

"Never mind about that," Chet said. He opened two beers and set them on the counter. "Once you get into bed, you can stay there three days if you want to." He came around the counter and sat on a stool. "Drink up and then I'll chauffeur you home."

"Let me ask you a question," Kermit said.

"Shoot. I know all the state capitals by heart and the names of every president up to McKinley."

"You're not keeping something back from me, are you?"

"How do you mean?"

"About Jossie. Agnes said she thought she was here in Kittredge. The way she had it, Jossie was due in today. Said you were supposed to meet her bus over in Weston. What about it?"

Chet took a long guzzle from his beer bottle, then set it down. "I knew I'd end up with my tail in a crack."

"Did she get here or not?"

"She got here all right. That was her perfume you smelled up at the house. She cleaned and scrubbed the whole place, made up the beds and everything."

"Where is she now?"

"I don't know. I thought she'd be there when I brought you back this afternoon. She didn't want me to tell you she was there. She wanted to surprise you."

"Then where did she get to?"

"You know as much as I do," Chet said.

"Maybe she went to her mother's place."

"That's what I thought. But she didn't. I strolled over there while you were having supper with Agnes. Her old lady was half in the bag so I snooped around the house a little. Jossie's not there. Nor her clothes either."

"You mean she came all the way down here to see me . . ."

"That's right."

". . . and now she's making herself scarce?"

"That's what it looks like," Chet said.

"Doesn't make sense."

"It does to me. She couldn't wait for you to get here, but at the same time she was scared to see you. I guess she chickened out."

When they started up the hill road on the motorcycle, the woods on both sides were dead black. The headlamp made a tight yellow tunnel in the darkness. Insects clouded around their heads and birds made anxious sounds in the night.

When Chet angled off the road and gunned his engine for the steep climb to the house he saw Jossie coming toward them, halfway down the slope. He slowed the motorcycle to a stop and cut the motor.

Fixed in the light-path like a moth, Jossie stumbled unevenly down the lane, carrying her suitcase in one hand. She came to a swaying stop at last, six feet from the motorcycle, full in the circle of light from the head-lamp. Her eyes focused imperfectly and her face was pale, but her mouth was trying to smile. And her voice when she spoke was unnaturally loud in the quiet dark. "Don't worry about me. I'm just fine. Not feeling a damned bit guilty over anything. Not about to kiss anybody's ass. If you don't want to like me, you don't have to. Tomorrow I'll be back in McKeesport. I got friends, you know. I'm not just some piece of nothing, waiting for somebody to decide whether . . . waiting to hear if . . ." Her eyes rolled back in her head then and she slumped slowly to the ground, soft and heavy as a sack of sugar.

II

"You think we ought to wake her up?" Chet said.

"*You* can if you want to. But not me," Kermit said. "With what she had to drink, I don't expect her to move around much till after the middle of the day."

Late in the morning, they were walking the high ridge, up-slope and east of the house, Spruce Knob off to their right, nosing up through the cloud cover. They carried rifles, slung loose in the crooks of their arms, their eyes taking in the mural of plants and flowers, trees and vines, birds, insects, and small ground-animals moving around them.

"I know what you mean about your dad," Chet said. He lit a cigarette and they hunkered down at the base of a tree. "But there's no use blaming him. It's not his fault the way things are."

"I just hate to think of her dying up here all by herself."

"So do I. But that's the way it is now. Half the houses around here, you go to the door and you find there's a woman living there by herself. Or with a kid or two maybe. A lot of the men just aren't around. They lit out for someplace or other. Looking for work. You can't blame them entirely."

"I don't. But that doesn't mean I have to like it. You

didn't like it when your folks took off, did you?"

"Course not. But I knew there was no stopping them."

"How do they like it out there?"

"They pretend to like it fine. To hear my sister tell it, California's the greatest place in the world. But I don't know. When I was out there a year or so ago, they seemed kinda antsy to me."

"They staying with Virgil?"

"In a way they are. He's got a little place outside of Guadalupe, and my folks are living at the back of his lot in a trailer."

"They sell the house here?"

"They tried to, but nobody wants it. So it's just sitting there, the window glass shot out, most of it, and shingles ripped off. It's a mess. This whole fucking territory's a mess, from the Virginia line all the way west to Brewster. Any man that's accustomed to working for wages is shit out of luck. It's all rocks in your bed and holes in your socks."

"You don't think things'll pick up?"

"Not a chance. We're out of business."

Kermit brought his rifle up, sighted carefully, and shot the cap off a toadstool thirty yards away. Chet shot at a cardinal high up in a beech tree and missed.

"Don't shoot a bird like that, you ass-hole."

"He's safe," Chet said. "I couldn't hit a heifer at that distance."

They stopped by a spring and flopped on their stomachs for a drink. When they stood up and started walking again, Kermit said, "I can't get over the change in you."

"How do you mean?"

"When I signed up in the army, you were laughing and scratching, had a college scholarship, you were going to fix everything."

"Yeah, well, I was eighteen. What do you know when you're eighteen?"

"I figured by the time you got out of school you'd have the whole country in first-class working order."

"Good thing you didn't put money on it."

"What happened?"

"How the hell do *I* know? Same thing that always happens, I guess. I kept asking questions nobody could answer."

"That was no reason to kick you out of school, was it?"

"*I* didn't think so. But when I asked *them* that, it turned out to be one of the questions they couldn't answer."

"You could have gone to a different school, couldn't you?"

"I guess so. But I decided it was a waste of time. If you don't have straight dice, it's no fun shooting craps. You know what I mean? It's pissing against the tide."

"It's better than giving up, isn't it?"

"I'm not giving up. I *gave* up."

"What the hell does that mean?"

"It means I'm tired of all the shit. I decided the thing to do is drink a lot."

"I can't believe what I'm hearing," Kermit said. "You're the one who always had the world by the ass."

Chet stopped walking and snapped his fingers. "Scratch out everything I just said. You are now looking at a man with a future. I will fly to Honolulu and become a bartender. Fifty dollars in tips every day, a swim in the ocean, and a different gray-haired lady every night. Then while they're sleeping I'll sneak out with their fur coats. I will be the number one gash man in Hawaii, a closet full of mink coats, and a smile for everybody."

12

When Kermit came into the house, Jossie was sitting at the kitchen table in a pajama top, coffee mug in her hands, the percolator just in front of her, steaming, resting on a bread board.

"Well, you didn't die," he said.

"You couldn't prove it by me."

He took a cup off the wall rack by the stove and sat down across the table from her. "Any coffee in there?"

"I made eight cups," she said. "At the rate I've been drinking it, I'd guess there's maybe a cup and a half left."

He poured himself a cup, put in a spoon of sugar and sampled it. Then he sugared in another half-spoon and settled square in his chair.

"I guess I'd better get some clothes on," she said.

"Why? You look all right to me."

"Maybe so from where you're sitting. But this is pajamas I'm wearing and I don't have on but the top half."

"I know all about it. Chet and I put it on you."

They looked at each other for a long moment. Then she said, "I'd just as soon you didn't gawk at me like that. It makes me feel funny."

"Why is that, do you suppose?"

"Well, I'm sitting on this cold chair with no pants on for one thing. Besides that, my head feels like there's a band concert playing inside it. And most of all, I'm not in any frame of mind to talk to you."

"Why'd you come all the way down here from Pennsylvania then?"

"That was yesterday," she said. "I had different ideas yesterday."

"Like what?"

"Like nothing. I don't know." She poured more coffee

in her cup. Then she said, "I guess I had some notion . . . you know what I was thinking. You got my letters, didn't you?"

He nodded his head.

"I got your answers, too," she said. "Tied them all up with rope. Had to rent an extra room to keep them in."

"You know me, I'm not much to write."

"No kidding."

He stirred his coffee carefully. Finally he said, "I was kind of mixed up in my own mind. I didn't know what to say. I thought it would be better to wait till I saw you."

"Like when?"

"Like now. When I got my time off."

"What made you think I'd be here?"

"I don't know. I just figured you might be."

"What if I hadn't been?" she said.

"I guess I'd have come up to McKeesport looking for you."

"Oh, come on, Kermit. You couldn't even scratch a couple lines on a postcard. You expect me to believe . . ."

"I don't care if you believe it. But that's what I had in my mind."

"Don't you think I know what you're doing? You figure you've got me on your hands so you might as well smooth things over till I leave."

"Suit yourself."

"Isn't that right?"

"Sure," he said. "You're always right. You've got a head like a God-damned walnut. A hard head and a big mouth. You've been the same since you were six years old. And you'll still be that way when you're eighty. Nobody can tell you anything because you already know it all."

"Does that mean you've got something to tell me?"

"No," he said.

"Then what's the difference?"

"There isn't any difference. Let's drop it."

"Talk about when *I* was six years old. You've been saying *that* since I was *four* years old. Whenever you get in a corner, when you don't know what to do, you always say, 'Let's drop it.'"

"That's what I mean," he said. "Let's drop it."

She got up and walked to the stove with the percolator, her bottom just showing under the pajama top.

"And cover up your ass, why don't you?"

"Why should I?" she said. "You've seen it before. Did you blindfold yourself when you put me to bed last night?"

"Well, you weren't much to look at. I promise you that."

"I've seen pictures of those German women. About two axe handles across the beam. Is that what you like now?"

She turned and walked away, into the downstairs bedroom. When she came out she was wearing jeans and a baggy sweatshirt. She sat down at the table again.

"Look," she said, "I don't want to hassle with you. You know how it's always been between you and me. We were together so long I just never thought about it being any different. When I came down here yesterday I thought there had to be some way we could patch things up. But I guess I was wrong. Because you've already made up your mind about things. I can see it in your face. So I'm not going to rag you anymore. But I'm not going to say I'm sorry either. I hate it about things not working out for us, but if what I did was more than you could stand, then maybe we never would have made it together anyhow. I admit it was a dumb-ass thing and it hurt everybody connected with it. Me most of all. But if you couldn't understand how I was feeling, what *made* me do it, then you don't know very much about me."

She got up and walked over to the window. She looked out for a moment, then turned back to face him.

"The only thing that kept me going that whole first hitch you did in the army was the thought that there was going to be an end to it, that when those three years were over, you'd be back. So when you came home last year I was so charged up I was almost crazy. My head was full of plans about all the things we could do together. I was so happy I was flying. And then to see you and have you tell me you'd re-enlisted, it just about tore me in two. All I could think was that you'd given up on us and that was the best way you knew to tell me. Maybe it sounds crazy now but that's how I felt. I didn't know what to do and I didn't know what to say. So I just ran. I guess I thought you'd follow me up to McKeesport. I know I hoped that's what you'd do. But you didn't. Next thing I knew, you'd gone back to Germany and I was mixed up and miserable. And to make things worse my folks were drinking and fighting every night, screaming at each other. I was ready to join a freak show. All I knew was I had to *do* something, *anything,* or I'd come apart. So I did the worst possible thing I could have done. I married somebody I didn't care anything about."

She came back to the table then and sat down. "For the worst reason in the world . . . to get even with you. I did it and I can't take it back. I was married for five weeks to a sweet, dumb man who didn't understand anything. He couldn't believe it when I said I'd marry him, and he couldn't believe it when I left. He was like an innocent bystander, one of those people you read about who gets hit by a stray bullet."

She stopped talking then, sat there looking down at her hands. Finally she said, "I don't know why I'm going over all this. Most of it I already told you when I wrote. I just can't leave it alone, I guess." She stood up again, pushed her chair in under the table. "When I came down here yesterday I was planning to do whatever I had to to get us back together again. But it didn't work. It doesn't make me feel very good, but I know when I'm licked. At least things won't be up in the air anymore."

She walked into the bedroom and closed the door behind her. A few minutes later, Kermit heard the outside bedroom door open and close. When he went to the window, he saw her cross the yard and turn down the lane toward town. In the bedroom, her suitcase was on the bed with a note pinned to it. "Chet. I'll be down at Mom's. Bring my bag down there when you get a chance. Jossie."

13

Chet sat on a kitchen chair tilted back against the wall, noodling on a guitar, night sounds outside, the owl and the frog and the crickets, the smell of fried pork sweet and smoky in the kitchen, leftovers from supper still on the table, windows open, curtains fluttering soft and silent in the breeze off the mountains, Kermit still at the table, legs up, leaning back, his feet resting on a chair seat, his hands behind his head.

Chet chorded, soft and tentative, then started to sing, husky, half-talk, half-whisper, conversational and nonmelodic, as if he was making it up a line at a time.

I said, "I'm cold and I'm hungry and I really need a job."
They said, "He sounds like a Communist to me."
I said, "The fish are gettin' poisoned from the garbage in the sea."
They said, "He sounds like a Communist to me."
I said, "There's fifteen million children who can't get enough to eat . . .
"The Indians are dying in the west . . .

"Somebody's chopping down the forest and clogging up the creeks . . .

"The smog is wreaking havoc with my chest."

I said, "My daddy needs a doctor and my baby needs some bread."

They said, "He sounds like a Communist to me."

I said, "I know I'm very lucky to be born in such a land . . . The home of the rich and the free."

They said, "He sounds like a Communist to me."

The melody trailed off in a series of floating atonal chords.

"Number one on the Hit Parade, New River State College, nineteen hundred and seventy-two," Chet said. "Year of our Lord and King Richard the Last, craphound supreme and ass-hole triumphant."

"Is that the kind of stuff got you blasted out of school?"

"Made me a hero with my fellow students. Idolized and pointed at. Spiritual leader and cult father to a family of twenty-year-old pussies."

". . . and got you kicked out of school."

"Right on my ass." He put down the guitar, stood up and stretched. "Where'd you hide the beer?"

"Out in the spring house."

"You want one?"

"Sure. Why not? We might as well get pissed. I'm on a furlough, for Christ's sake."

Chet came back with two cold and dripping bottles of beer, handed one to Kermit, and twisted off the cap on his own. "Down the hatch," he said. He tilted the bottle up and drank half of it before he set it down. "I guess this don't taste like much after the beer you get over there in Germany."

"No, I guess not."

"What's it like, living in a strange country? Different

people and a different language and everything."

"Well . . . it ain't what it's cracked up to be."

"How do you mean?"

"The army's the army. Whether you're in Wiesbaden or Kansas doesn't make a hell of a lot of difference. The food's the same. The beds are the same. The officers and the barracks, they all look alike, one place or another."

"You get some time off, don't you?"

"Sure. But after two or three weekends in the same town, that gets old too. You see the same guys you see all week, stumbling around with their shirt-tails out, looking for some kind of action, getting drunk, trying to get laid."

"I hear those German girls are really fruit for Americans."

"Not that I've ever seen. They've all got jobs and money of their own. They don't need any hand-outs from a bunch of sad-assed soldiers. Those days are over. Most of the guys don't even leave the post when they have time off. They shoot pool and play poker and that's about it."

"Doesn't sound like much of a life."

"It's not. It's a living. That's all. You put in your twenty years, then sit back and collect that monthly check."

"Is that what you're fixing to do?"

"Damned if I know. One day I think one thing, the next day something else. When I left Frankfurt a few days ago, I had it in mind to sweat out my two more years, then pack it in. But now I don't know."

"What changed your mind?"

"I didn't say I'd changed my mind."

"Don't horse-shit me, Kermit. I can see through you like a window glass. You figured things were going to work out different for you and Jossie, didn't you?"

"How do you mean?"

"You know what I mean. You figured she'd be waiting here and the two of you would patch things up. Isn't that right?"

"I don't know," Kermit said. "I thought it might work out, I guess."

"Then why didn't it?"

"Don't ask me. Ask her."

"I don't have to ask her. I *know* what she wants. She didn't make the trip down here for nothing."

"Maybe no," Kermit said, "but you don't see her around, do you?"

"For Christ's sake, Kermit. I can't decide if you're dumb or just bull-headed. What the hell did you expect? She's got some pride, too, the same as you have. Why do you think she got herself drunk last night? That's not like Jossie and you know it. She was scared to death of what you might say when you saw her, scared shitless you wouldn't want her around anymore."

Chet pushed back from the table, got up, and went outside. He came back with two more bottles of beer. "Look," he said, "don't get the wrong idea. I'm not trying to hustle you. It's no skin off me if you and Jossie get together or not. If you don't want to start up with her again, that's up to you. All I'm saying is this. If you *do* want her around, if you came back here with the idea of getting things straightened out between you two, then you're sure as hell playing your cards wrong. She's made all the moves she can make. Now it's up to you."

14

After midnight, dark and silent in Kittredge, Kermit stopped by a high hedge in front of Clara Floyd's house. There was no sound, no lights at the windows. He moved easily across the grass to the porch, staying in the shadow of the house.

At the edge of the front porch he pressed against the siding, one hand on the porch rail, tried to see through the screen door into the living room.

Suddenly he heard a hollow thump and a man's voice, low and husky. "God damn it, Clara. You like to snapped my arm off at the wrist."

"Shhh. Keep quiet."

"What are you doing?"

"I lost my balance."

"Get back up here where I can take hold of you."

"Shhh."

"Jesus Christ, what are you pinching me for?"

"I told you to stay quiet. Jossie's upstairs asleep."

"Just slide over here," the man said.

"There. How's that?"

"That's more like it."

Kermit eased away from the porch and around the side of the house. He tried the kitchen door. It was open. He slipped inside and up the back stairs, stayed close to the wall so the floor boards wouldn't creak, and found the door to Jossie's bedroom. Turning the knob slowly, he gentled the door open, moved across the room, and sat down easily on the edge of the bed. He put his hand on her shoulder and when she woke up suddenly, he put his other hand over her mouth.

"Don't say anything. It's me."

He took his hand away then. Before she could speak he said, "Just put a coat on over your pajamas and come along up to the house. We'll get your stuff tomorrow."

"Where's Mom?"

"She's having a party on the front-room couch. She won't hear anything."

They moved quietly along the hall, down the back

stairs, and out through the kitchen door. They angled across two back yards and came out on the hill road. Kermit stopped and put his arms around her. He stood there holding her against him for a long time. Then he took her hand and they walked up the road toward his house.

They could hear Chet's breathing, even and deep, in the downstairs bedroom as they crossed the kitchen. Jossie climbed the ladder to the sleeping loft with Kermit just behind her. She stood by the window while he lowered the trap door and slid the bolt.

He came over to her, put his arms around her and kissed her. She trembled against him.

"Are you cold?" he said.

"No."

"You want to keep your pajamas on?"

"No."

He took her coat and draped it across a chair back. Then he turned her to him and took her pajamas off, the pants first, then the jacket. They stood facing each other in the soft light coming through the window, and she began to unbutton his shirt.

When he was naked, she put her arms around him and pressed her face close against his chest.

"God, I missed you so much," she said.

"Then what's all those tears for?"

"I don't know."

"Are you laughing or crying?"

"I don't know. Both, I guess."

Part Two

15

The front of Clara Floyd's house was pale yellow in the morning light. Sun rays slanted through the trees, across the porch, through the slits in the window shade, and made a pattern of irregular stripes across her face as she lay on her back on the couch, her cotton dress wrinkled and unbuttoned down the front, her blue half-slip hiked up to her waist, her legs and feet bare, her run-over slippers looking broken on the floor. And an uneven circle of empty beer cans around the couch.

There was a sound then, abrupt and mechanical, from the back of the house, from the side yard perhaps, from somewhere. Clara shuddered, her arm flopped over the couch edge, and she opened her eyes.

Only her eyes gave a clue as to what she had looked like twenty years before. They were round and blue and innocent, like the china eyes of a mail-order doll. Watery now, rimmed with pink, flat and furtive, they still retained, somehow, a hint of some former prettiness.

The rest of her face was old beyond its years, puffy from too much sleep and not enough rest, from cigarettes and beer, bad food, and white mule. Her lipstick was smeared and rubbed into the skin around her mouth and her teeth were a disaster of bad genes and worse care. Her hair was clumsily bleached and scorched frizzy by a careless permanent. Imitation-gold horseshoes dangled from her ears and a green metal shamrock hung around her neck on a silver chain.

She pulled herself together now with a groan and began the slow process of getting to her feet. Torso vertical, feet on the floor, hair pushed back from her forehead, a kicking aside of the nearest beer cans, and she was up, unsure, unsteady, but moving toward the window.

She pulled the curtains to one side and looked out around the edge of the paper blind. In the yard, at the roadside, Chet was loading Jossie's suitcase into the motorcycle sidecar. As he kicked the engine to life and rode off, Jossie walked back across the grass toward the kitchen door. Coming up the steps and into the kitchen, she found her mother stuffing twists of paper and scraps of kindling into the wood stove.

"Well, I'm up," Clara said, "but I don't know why. I didn't sleep worth a darn."

"Maybe if you crawled into bed, you'd sleep better than you do on that broken-down couch."

"Oh, I've tried that. But it doesn't help. When my curse is due, I start to get the sick headache and I can't get a wink of sleep no matter what."

"That's a shame."

"Sometimes a beer and a cigarette will do the trick. Make me drowsy, I mean. Cliff got me a six-pack last night over at Dude's and he was good enough to sit with me while I drank one or two but it didn't help a particle. I just laid there staring at the ceiling the whole blessed night." She measured coffee and water into the percolator and lit a cigarette from the butt of the one she'd just finished.

"You want me to fix you some breakfast?" Jossie said. "Why don't you pump out some water and wash up a little while I fry some bacon and a couple eggs."

"Ohh, don't mention food to me. Not when I'm all dragged out like this. I can't get a bite down. Just black coffee. That's the rinctum. Have me good as new in half an hour."

Jossie sat down with her forearms resting on the table and watched her mother move around the kitchen, her bare feet making a gritty sound on the linoleum. Each time she dragged on her cigarette she coughed, dry and rasping. Smoke trailed across her face and ashes snowed down lightly on the front of her dress, on the stove, the floor, and the tabletop. Finally she poured some coffee, ink-black and steaming, into a cracked mug and lowered herself into a chair.

"Jesus, my head's about to bust. You don't have any aspirin, do you?"

"I'll walk over to the store and get you some if you want."

"No. Don't make a special trip."

"I'm going anyway," Jossie said. "I have to buy some stuff."

"What kind of stuff?"

"Groceries mostly."

Clara took a scalding gulp of coffee, dragged deep on her cigarette, and squinted at Jossie through the smoke.

"I thought you were heading back up to McKeesport. Ain't that what you told me yesterday evening?"

"I changed my mind."

"When you fixing to go then?"

"I'm not. Not till Kermit has to report back."

"He changed your mind for you. Is that it?"

"No. I changed my own mind."

"But he helped you, I bet."

Jossie smiled and said, "I guess you could say that."

"I knew there was something up. I looked in your room late last night and you weren't there."

"I was there till after midnight. Then Kermit came after me."

Clara shook her head. "I never figured out what you see in that shite-poke. It was bad enough when you were a kid. But now you're . . . what are you, nineteen?"

"Twenty."

"Twenty years old. And you've never seen anybody you cotton to more than him?"

"No, I haven't."

"You had a good husband if you ask me. Fred Baines is a man any woman could be proud of. If he ain't got what it takes to keep a woman happy, I miss my guess."

"Maybe you ought to look him up then," Jossie said.

"Don't talk smart to me."

"He's closer to your age than he is to mine."

"Oh, listen to that, will you? You're not gonna be twenty all your life, Miss Pretty-Pants. And I guarantee you, a few years from now, you'll be a sorry girl you didn't hang onto Fred Baines. Thinking about all the time you wasted on you-know-who."

"I don't think so."

"Course you don't. Cause you can't see three feet past your nose. You think you owe him something? Just because he got you off in the bushes when you were barely old enough to even be with a man? You think that gives him some kind of hold on you? Well, it doesn't. He doesn't own you. Looks like to me he doesn't even want you around. Otherwise he'd act different. If you ask me . . ."

"Nobody's asking you, Mom."

"Maybe not, but I'm telling you anyhow. He's like any

other man. He likes to have a little hometown diddle when he gets back on furlough once a year. And after that's said, it's *all* said."

"Maybe you're right," Jossie said. She pushed her chair back and stood up from the table.

"I saw Chet hauling your clothes off. I suppose that means you'll be laying around up at the Docker place the rest of the time you're here."

"Something like that."

"Don't you care what people think about you?"

"What people?"

"People here in Kittredge. Folks you knew all the time you were growing up."

"Who cares what they think? *You* don't care, do you?"

"I most certainly do. This is my home. I have to live here."

"You mean you don't want me to do anything to hurt your reputation?"

"That's right. That's what *I'm* thinking about and you ought to be, too."

Jossie walked to the door of the living room, looked at the beer cans on the floor, the stained and sagging sofa under the front window. Then she turned back to her mother and said, "I promise you one thing, Mom. When I leave Kittredge your reputation will be just as good as it is now."

16

Clara Floyd had it wrong about Jossie and Kermit. She assumed that Jossie, since she was three years younger, had been, in some sense, a victim. There was logic in that assumption but it was wrong nonetheless. Jossie was not seduced and abandoned. But she had been abandoned. At least in her own mind. And that abandonment brought about a seduction. But not hers. Kermit's.

One summer afternoon when she was twelve, discovered by her mother in her room, door shut, windows down, August heat burning through the roof, she lay on her back on the bed and refused to move.

"I don't want to go outdoors. I don't want to go anyplace."

"Mitzi and Arloa came over ten minutes ago looking for you. I didn't know you were home. It's sure no kind of a day to bake yourself up here under the rafters. Why don't you go on over to Mitzi's and stir up some lemonade or something?"

"I don't want any lemonade. And I don't want to go to Mitzi's."

"Why not?"

"Because she's *dumb.* And Arloa along with her. Mitzi's dumb and Arloa's dumber. I have to see them when I'm in school. That's bad enough. But I don't have to listen to them running off at the mouth all summer."

"You're not fooling anybody," Clara said then.

"I'm not trying to."

"Yes, you are. You've been moping around here all summer long, morning till night. Can't get a lick of work out of you. Or a civil word. Acting like you lost your best friend. But I know what's in your head. Your nose is out of joint because you can't run with the boys any more."

"I don't know what you're talking about."

"Yes, you do. I'm talking about Kermit and Chet. You've been tagging after them since you were five years old. Tom-boying along, more boy than girl. Now all of a sudden they've got other fish to fry and you don't like it."

"Who says so?"

"*I* say so. They're three or four years older than you. You have to remember that. They're turning into men and you're just a kid yet."

"I can do anything they can do."

"No, you can't either," Clara said. "Not by a long shot. They're looking for a different kind of fun now. Take my word for it. And you don't fit in. You're not big enough and you're not old enough. And thank God for that. Otherwise we'd be likely to have a woods-colt around here by Easter time."

"I don't know what you're talking about."

"Yes, you do. You know what those two have been up to all summer. Everybody around here knows. They're out there at the quarry every afternoon, stripped off and rolling around in the grass with that feeble-minded daughter of Cass McCabe's. If you don't believe me, ask your brother, Jack. He told his dad about it."

"I don't believe anything Jack says."

"It's the truth all right. He's not the only one who says it." Clara shook the foot of the bed. "Now, are you going to get up out of there or do I have to tote you?"

Some pastel transformation floated behind Jossie's eyes. She sat up on the bed and said, "Maybe I'll walk over to Mitzi's house after all."

Late that afternoon, a mile or so outside of Kittredge, Jossie lay flat on her stomach under a thick tangle of dewberry bushes, forty feet back from the edge of the quarry, watching, listening, waiting uneasily for she wasn't sure what. She could hear voices, and splashing, and every few minutes Chet or Kermit climbed up out of the water to the stone lip of the quarry, poised there, white and gleaming wet, and dived in again.

At last they scrambled out and lay flat on the grass in the sun with Ella McCabe, short and fat, red hair and flat blue eyes, great heavy breasts and no hair at all on her body, on her back between them, pink and giggling, babbling non-stop in some peculiar cadence, making sounds that resembled real words but were in fact only sounds.

Scarcely breathing, almost near enough to touch them, her face burning with shame and apprehension and some other unfamiliar heat, Jossie lay motionless, her mouth dry, her hands damp suddenly, and watched Chet and Kermit, in turn, roll up on the soft mass of Ella, her arms and legs wrapped around their bodies, her hips heaving and pumping under them, her baby voice squealing and giggling in the stillness by the quarry pool.

Each boy, on his knees, watched as the other took his turn. As one withdrew, red-faced, and flopped to one side, the other took his place, no lost motion. And Ella, eyes closed, undulated without pause, self-involved, out of control, marking no change, it seemed, between one fifteen-year-old erection and the other.

It went on like that for a long time, slow and violent, till the giggles turned to ugly, painful groans, till the boys hung limp and raw. Ella's stomach churned still, she twitched like a dying animal, and her eyes rolled back white in her head. But she felt nothing now. She lay in the sun like a traffic victim, Kermit and Chet sprawled wet and heavy across her, a tangle of white bodies in the burning heat at the edge of the quarry.

That night and the three days following were agonizing for Jossie. All her choices frightened her. But the prospect of being left behind while Kermit raced ahead to wherever it was he was going was the most frightening of all.

She went looking for him, finally, intercepted him one early evening as he walked down the hill road from his house to town.

"Where you going?" he said.

"Right here. I came looking for you." She fell in beside him and they walked on down the road.

"Where you been? I haven't seen you."

"I've been where I always am," she said.

"Well, I haven't seen anything of you."

"I guess that's cause you spend most of your time up at the quarry."

"No, I don't," he said quickly. "I'm working part-time down at the lumber-yard. You know that. That's where I am most days."

"And soon as you get off work you high-tail it out to the quarry."

"Chet and I take a swim every chance we get. Feels good after you've been working in the heat."

"I'm not talking about swimming," she said. "I'm talking about what else you do up there at the quarry."

"Like what?"

"Like wallering around bare-assed with that half-wit McCabe girl."

Kermit stopped walking. "Who said anything like that?"

"*I* say it. Everybody says it. It's the truth."

"Like hell it is. People are always talking about her, saying she screws anybody that asks her. But that doesn't mean me."

"Is that a fact?"

"Yes. It's a fact."

"Bull-shit, Kermit. I *saw* you. Three days ago. You and Chet. Naked as a bird's ass and laying all over that poor fat girl like she was something special."

"What do you mean, you *saw* us?"

"I mean I *saw* you. I was close enough to spit on you. I can tell you who took the first turn and how many times you did it. I was right there in the bushes and I didn't miss a lick."

"I don't believe you."

"You better believe me. It's the truth. If you give me a pencil I'll draw you a picture."

"Jesus, you ought to be ashamed of yourself."

"*Me?* What about you? You're the one that ought to be ashamed. You and Chet both. That girl's nothing but a piece of meat. She can't spell her name or count to five. I mean can't you do any better than that? Is she the best you can get?"

"Don't worry about me."

"I'm *not* worrying about you. I feel sorry for you. Because you'll settle for *anything,* it looks like. Next thing you know, they'll catch you in somebody's sheep pen."

"If I was you, young lady, I'd keep my nose out of things I don't know anything about."

"I admit I don't know anything about it. But you don't either. If you did, you wouldn't be slobbering over Ella McCabe the way you are, taking turns with Chet like it was some kind of shooting gallery at a county fair."

He started to say something, then stopped, and she said, "You see? You don't have an answer, do you? You know I'm right."

"The hell I do." He turned and started down the road again, Jossie keeping up with him. They walked the rest of the way in silence till they stopped in front of her house.

She looked up at him then and said, "I thought you liked me. We've liked each other since I was in third grade."

"That's different," he said. "This is different."

"No, it's not. I may not be the size of a milk cow like Ella but I'm a girl just as much as she is. I can do anything to you that she can do. I was watching her. I can do all that."

"You don't know what you're talking about, Jossie. You're still a kid."

"No, I'm not. I'm twelve now. Mom was only two years older than me when she had my brother. And what about *you?* You're barely fifteen, for Pete's sake." She pulled his head down and kissed him. Then she said, "Seems to me all that stuff would be a lot more fun with somebody you liked. Did you stop liking me? Is that it?"

"No. That's not it."

"Good. That's all I need to know. You've got a little head-start on me but I'll catch up. And I guarantee you, you won't need to run after Ella McCabe any more."

She was right. On both counts. She *did* catch up. And Kermit never saw Ella McCabe again.

17

Gabe Christopher, a gaunt man in his fifties, gray hair clipped short, hands deep in the pockets of faded bib overalls, an army fatigue cap on the back of his head, ambled across the porch of Jernegan's store and looked off up the road. A state police car was slowly rolling toward him. "Here comes the bird dog," he said.

A half step behind him on the porch, Russell Bippus, his eyes small behind dime-store spectacles, skin pale and freckled, belly hanging low and heavy over the top of his pants, squinted up the road. "You reckon he gets as much as he says he does?"

"Whether he does or not, I guarantee you it's more than anybody else around here is getting. With Jim it's like a business. He *works* at it."

The car pulled over and stopped in front of the store, the door on the driver's side opened, and Jim August swung his legs out from under the wheel, stood up tall, and stretched himself in the sun. Twenty-seven years old, he was lean and flat-muscled in the snug-fitting trooper's uniform, boots gleaming, gun belt around his hips, wide-brimmed hat cocked low over his eyes. He adjusted his crotch lovingly and leaned back against the hood of the car, ankles crossed, arms folded across his chest. "What's new, boys?"

"Nothing new around here," Gabe said. "Only excitement we got is wagering who's gonna go home with

Clara Floyd on any particular night."

"Who was it last night?" Jim said.

"Couldn't prove it by me. I was in a game of hearts up at my brother-in-law's. Who'd she give it up to last night, Russ?"

"Cliff Sensibaugh. At any rate, he left the store with her. Had a six-pack under each arm."

"There's your answer. Old Cliff cut the pie last night."

"Didn't think he had it in him," Jim said.

"You don't know Cliff. He'd fuck a lawn mower if the blades wasn't too sharp."

"What about you, Jimbo?" Gabe sat down on the edge of the porch. "Anybody work you over last night?"

Jim grinned and tilted his hat against the sun. "You got me wrong, boys. I'm no snatch-hound. What if I was to tell you I sat home all last night, watching the box and eating Ritz crackers?"

"I'd say 'horse-shit.' We know you. Who was she?"

"Well . . . I don't think I ought to tell any names. But I'll give you a couple hints. She's a little widow woman, lives on the county gravel a mile or so east of Brindle."

"Brindle?" Gabe said. "I don't know a damned soul over there."

"Sure you do," Jim said. "I'll give you another clue."

Russell chuckled. "Hell, this beats a quiz show, Gabe. We're liable to win ourselves a Dodge Dart or something."

"She's got red hair," Jim went on, "and she was the Princess of the Berry Festival a few years back . . ."

"Wait a minute now. I think maybe I know who you mean," Gabe said. "That sounds like Carol . . . what the hell's her name? Her dad's an auctioneer, travels all over this end of the state . . . Ed something or other. Ed Gustafson! Carol Gustafson! Is that the one?"

Jim smiled like a raccoon.

"I remember her now," Russell said. "She's the one

looks like her motor's running day and night."

"You better believe it," Jim said.

"She sure as hell ain't no widow woman," Gabe said. "She's the one that's married to the government man, ain't she?"

"News to me," Jim said. "Told me she was a widow."

"Widow, my ass. She's married to a farm agent. Goes on the road for the state. From Virginia all the way to the Ohio line."

"I don't know why she'd fib to me," Jim said.

"Listen to him, will you?" Gabe said. "Like a cat licking the cream separator."

"Well," Russell said. "How *was* she?"

Jim fished a cigarette out of his shirt pocket, tucked it in the corner of his mouth, and lit it. "Well, boys, all I can say is, she like to put me out of commission. For starters, when I got there, she came to the door in one of those nightgowns you can see through. Dinner on the plate."

"Jesus Christ."

"And if you remember from the Berry Festival, you know she's got some shape on her." He took a slow drag on his cigarette. "I never even had a chance to get my gun belt off. Soon as I came through the door she sat me down on a kitchen chair and straddled me like I was a Shetland pony. Pushed those big soft titties against my face and bounced up and down like a kid on a teeter-totter, laughing her head off and squealing like a stuck hog!"

"She really went for it, huh?"

"Couldn't get her stopped. She humped me all over the house. Upstairs, downstairs, you name it. Must have been three in the morning before she ran down a little and we got some sleep."

"Son-of-a-bitch."

"Then this morning she was up early. Brought me a

cup of coffee in bed and when I got up she fixed me some fried chicken . . ."

"For breakfast?"

"That's right. A whole plate of it. And then some apple pie with heavy cream. And a couple cold beers to polish it off."

"Man, oh man," Russell said.

"Then when I was fixing to leave, hat on and the whole works, she pulled up her skirt, wrapped her legs around me, and we knocked one off standing up, right inside the front door."

"Ain't that something, though? Gives me a bone-on just hearing about it."

"It's the truth," Jim said.

"You sure have a rough life," Russell said.

"I'm what you call a public servant."

"Public *stud* is more like it," Gabe said.

Jim chuckled, dropped his cigarette in the dust, and ground it under his heel. As he looked off up the street, Jossie left her mother's house, carrying a bag of groceries, and headed in the opposite direction, toward the hill road.

"That's not Jossie, is it?" Jim said.

Gabe turned and looked. "That's her, all right."

"I thought she was up in Pennsylvania someplace."

"She was. But now she's back."

"No use slow-talking her," Russell said. "She's got her hands full up at the Docker place."

18

As Jossie turned up the woods road leading to Kermit's house, the police car pulled up even with her, rolled beside her as she walked.

"Want a lift?" Jim said.

"It's all right. I'm not going far."

"Might as well save some wear and tear on your feet. Where you heading?"

"Up to the Docker place."

"Climb in. I'll have you there in two shakes."

He leaned across the front seat and swung the car door open. Jossie slid in, pulled the door shut, and settled the bag of groceries on her lap. Jim let the motor idle, one arm stretched across the seat-back, the other resting on the steering wheel. "Surprised to see you. I thought you were long gone."

"Bad penny . . ."

"Last time I pulled into that truck-stop over at Dunstan I asked what had become of you, but nobody seemed to know. Or else they weren't saying."

"I went back up to Pennsylvania to keep house for my Dad."

"I know. That's what I found out later. Ran into your mother over at Dude's. And she told me. I was sorry to hear your folks split up."

"Yeah, well . . . that's what they wanted to do."

He offered her a cigarette and lit one himself. "I sure hated to see you leave Dunstan. I had the idea you and I were just about to set off a few sparks together."

"It's news to me."

"Maybe so. But all the same, it was a feeling I had."

"Listen," she said. "Maybe I'd better walk after all. I'm in kind of a hurry."

"No sweat." He put the car in gear and rolled slowly up the hill road. Steering with one hand, his right arm still draped across the back of the seat, he said, "Well, I have to say this much. You're pretty as ever."

"You never saw a girl that didn't look pretty to you."

"Don't kid yourself. The only ones that look pretty to

me are the pretty ones. Like the fella says, there's too many fish in the creek."

"That's what I heard."

"They tell me your old boyfriend came back. All the way from Germany, they said. Just to see you."

"They got it wrong. His mother died a few weeks ago. That's the main reason he's home."

"Maybe so. But I bet he was anxious to see you, too."

"I hope so."

He glanced down at the groceries on her lap. "Looks like you're laying in supplies. I guess your friend won't be lonesome while he's here."

"I guess not. Not if I can help it."

"Surprises me a little," he said, "to hear you talk like that. The way you acted up in Dunstan, those truck drivers were laying bets you'd end up as a nun someplace."

"Is that a fact?"

"Don't give me that. You know it as well as *I* do. You were giving the cold shoulder to everybody, including yours truly. We all figured you wanted nothing to do with a man."

Jossie looked directly at him, gave him a sugary smile, and said, "I don't know where you got *that* idea. I go to bed with anybody that asks me. Just as long as they ask me *nice.*"

"Sure you do. Like hell you do."

He turned up the sharp incline just below the Docker house. "What I'm trying to say is, I think you could do a little better for yourself in the *man* department."

"Did you have anybody particular in mind?"

He grinned and said, "The hills are full of prime stock."

"Like you, for instance?"

"Could be. I don't want to blow my own horn, but if you ask around you might get a good report."

As they pulled up and stopped in front of the house, Chet and Kermit came out of the barn at the far side of the cattle pens and walked toward the car.

Jossie got out of the car, closed the door behind her, then leaned down and talked to Jim through the open window. "You think maybe I should walk away from Kermit and start up with you . . . is that it?"

"Why not? I could show you a good time. There's no question about *that.*"

She looked over her shoulder at Kermit walking toward her, still forty yards away, then turned back to Jim. "All right," she said. "Tell you what I'll do. I'll ask Kermit. If he says it's all right with him, I'll do it."

Jim sat behind the wheel and watched her walk away. When she met Kermit and Chet at the corner of the house, she started talking to them. They looked across the yard toward the car. Then she smiled and said something else and the three of them started to laugh.

Jim felt his cheeks turn hot. He put the car in reverse, turned around, and drove back down the hill.

19

From his early childhood in Parkersburg, no one had questioned that Jim August was blessed with natural gifts. He had good health, strong bones, and a quick mind. His parents were prosperous and sensible. They managed to make each of their five children, two boys and three girls, feel valuable. They were taught how to study, how to work, and how to make social compromises without sacrificing their identities. Each child learned early that his key responsibility was to himself, that his life-choices would be his own.

Jim had a fine time growing up. At home and in school.

He developed self-confidence and a pleasant manner. Achievement came easy. People noticed him and liked him.

Gradually, then, commencing when he was sixteen, as he started to take more specific control of his life, the pattern changed. He began to make odd choices. In a few surprising months some emotional imperative transformed him from what he had been to something no one had imagined he could be, a difficult young man. Positive forces crackled from pole to pole and turned negative. He was dismissed from school teams, suspended from classes, and asked to leave people's homes. He abandoned his friends and found new ones, mostly older than he, in the sorriest neighborhoods of Parkersburg. He was cited for traffic violations and arrested at last for driving drunk. His father, of course, arranged for his release. But when he was arrested again, four days later, no one interceded. After three weeks in jail, Jim visited his parents and explained their shortcomings to them in profane detail. Then he got into his car and left Parkersburg.

Nearly seven years later he came back, handsome, apparently prosperous, and openly critical of his former mistakes. He agreed to spend a few weeks in his parents' home while he scouted about for a place of his own. No one who saw him doubted that he had come full circle, that he was himself again.

Six weeks passed. After a high-intensity courtship he married Sue Marie Englund, the only daughter of Webb Englund, publisher of the *Parkersburg Sentinel* and the *Wheeling Times* and owner of sixteen radio stations in Ohio and West Virginia.

Englund produced the most conspicuous wedding Parkersburg could remember, then sent the couple off on a two-month wedding trip to Greece, Italy, and Yugoslavia. When they returned he presented them with a fine old house on the river, four servants in residence, two cars in the garage. Sue Marie was three months pregnant now. And divinely happy, she told her girl friends. But she was strangely silent.

Five weeks after returning home, having cancelled a downtown luncheon appointment and come back to the house early, she found her husband naked on the living room floor with Ulla Tagg, their cook, a fifty-year-old German woman from Munich.

Sue Marie ran upstairs, locked herself in the bathroom, and called her father. When he arrived at the house twenty minutes later, she told him the details of her honeymoon trip. They left the house together, and she waited in the car while Englund beat Jim senseless on the lawn beside the garage.

Next morning, Sue Marie and her parents left for the Caribbean. Six weeks later, she was divorced and no longer pregnant.

By that time, Jim August had made another odd decision. He'd driven to Charleston and made application for admission to the State Police Academy. Recognizing his natural gifts, they accepted him at once.

In a few weeks, Jim had put Sue Marie permanently out of his mind. But he never forgot her father.

20

Chet sat cross-legged on the kitchen floor, back against the wall, picking out a single-string melody line on his guitar. Kermit and Jossie were still at the table.

"What about your dad?" Kermit said.

"He's in Chicago. That's all I know," Jossie said. "After Mom left at Christmastime, he stayed on in McKeesport till April. Like I told you, I quit my job in Dunstan and went up to keep house for him so he wouldn't be by himself. But then he got laid off where he was working and he decided to head up north and try to get something there."

"That doesn't sound like him. Not to write or be in touch with you at all."

"Well, I don't know. He's changed a lot. It's close to four years now since we left Kittredge and the factory work has changed him. Being inside and all. He hates it. And that cat-fighting with Mom didn't do him any good either. In some ways, I guess he was relieved when she finally up and left. But he missed her, too. They'd been married for more than twenty years. And whatever else anybody thinks about Mom, you have to admit she's got a way about her. No matter where she goes, drunk or sober, there's always a flock of men around. It seemed to me Dad got five years older in just those few months after she left. Then we started hearing stories about how she was carrying on down here . . ."

Chet struck a full chord, cleared his throat, and said, "Hold it down, folks. The program is about to start." He stared at them, mock-serious, and vamped till he had their full attention. Then he began to sing. Slowly. Feeling his way.

> When I racked up my bike,
> I was bleeding in the dirt.
> The doctor looked me over,
> And he said, "I think you're hurt."
> He said, "I'm awful sorry,
> But there's nothing I can do.
> Your Blue Cross ran out,
> And your Blue Shield too."
> So I say, "Bring back the Hippocratic Oath.
> The doctors won't work till after they're paid.
> Bring back the Hippocratic Oath.
> The doctors get rich and the patients get daid!"

When he struck a final chord and put his guitar down, Jossie said, "You turned into quite a singer, Chet."

"Sings like a bird," Kermit said.

"More like a duck," Chet said. "Just like a duck in the mating season." He got up and leaned his guitar in the corner. "A duck that's getting ready to hatch a bunch of little ducks." He did a clumsy time-step over to the porch door, opened the screen and said, "Good night, folks."

"You're heading the wrong way," Jossie said. "The bedroom's right in there."

"If it's all the same to you, I think I'll roll up in a blanket in the barn."

"What's the sense of that?" Kermit said.

"Self-preservation. I don't want to get trampled on in case you two come down from upstairs and start chasing each other." He was out the door then. The screen slammed shut behind him.

Jossie crossed to the doorway and called after him. "Chet, you're crazy. You can't sleep out there in the straw." She turned to Kermit. "Go bring him back. The mice will chew him to pieces."

Kermit got up and came over to the door. "It's all right. Let him go. He's crazy but he's trying to be nice."

Jossie put her arm around his waist. "Are you going to chase me around the house like he said?"

"Not unless I have to."

21

When Chet mentioned that his wife's name was Sarah, he was telling the truth. Everything else he said about her was distorted.

Her full name was Sarah Ainslie Wiggam. Her father was Howard Ainslie. He had inherited a Minnesota timber fortune and quadrupled it in Chicago real estate.

Sarah had been married only once, to David Wiggam, a pleasant, gangling man, third son of a family whose ancestors had settled Rhode Island. After a shaky start as a bond salesman and a journalist in Providence, and one semester as a Greek teacher at Brown, David pulled himself together and picked up steam. He studied the intricacies of real estate manipulation with his father-in-law, moved south, and applied what he had learned to the undeveloped swamps of Florida.

For the last twenty-eight years of their thirty-year marriage, David and Sarah lived, childless but well-mated, in Palm Beach, accumulating wealth, sailing their boat in the Atlantic, and drinking too much. At age fifty-six, David's liver gave out and he died.

Four years later, when she was fifty-nine, Sarah married Chet. As reported by him, they did meet in a bar. But it was Chet who was the pursuer, not Sarah. "You may not be too young for me," she said, "but I'm sure as hell too old for you."

Apparently she was wrong about that. Some soft and cultured, full-bosomed, expensive-smelling aspects of her were very much right for Chet. Unable to persuade her or to insinuate himself into her life in any deft or sophisticated way, he broke down her resistance by sheer, stubborn persistence.

"God, you're unreal," she said. "With all that energy you could bring a stone to life."

With her eyes open, determined to stay in control of the situation, she gradually lost control. She drank with him, spent time with him, and, inevitably, went to bed with him. And finally she married him.

Searching for solid ground then, for some new rules for a new life, she decided to solve whatever difficulties might arise by refusing to recognize them. She simply treated Chet the same way she had treated David. Solve problems, make a home, keep things nice. He was a man, she was a woman, they were married. "Simplistic foolishness," she told herself. But it worked.

In spite of over thirty years' difference in their ages, there was nothing maternal in her feelings for him. His relentless physical enjoyment of her would not permit it. No space or time for that. So she manipulated her feelings, simply turned her mind off, postponed all judgments. Too wise to imagine it could last forever, she was also too sensible not to enjoy it for as long as it might last.

Chet told her, early on, about Kermit and Jossie. Lied to her about Jossie as he'd lied to himself since he was sixteen. But Sarah was not deceived.

Finally he told her everything, things and feelings he'd never admitted to anyone, and it was Sarah who persuaded him to go back to Kittredge.

"What good will that do?" he said.

"I can't answer that."

"Then what's the point?"

"The point is you can't spend the rest of your life hung up on a *maybe*. You can't keep this girl curled up inside of you forever. If you want her, you have to try for her. God knows I've never seen you shy about anything else you wanted."

"This is different," Chet said.

"Sure it is. It's always *different* when it hurts."

"I mean Jossie is Kermit's girl."

"Then why did she marry somebody else?"

"I don't know. But whatever the reason was, it didn't change the way she feels about Kermit. I'll make you a bet on that."

"She sounds like a ding-bat."

"She's nuts about Kermit, that's all. She always has been."

"Then you'd better forget about her."

"I know that," he said. "That's what I told *you.*"

"Either that or do something about it."

"Like what?"

"Go back home. Go see your friend when he comes home on furlough. You'll find out in a hurry what's going on. If he doesn't want her or if she doesn't want him, then at least you've got a chance. After he goes back, tell her how you feel. The worst that can happen is you get turned down. At least that's something definite. Better than what you've got now."

Chet sat looking at her. "I don't understand you," he said.

"Sure you do."

"No, I don't. You're talking to me like my aunt or something. Like there's nothing between us at all."

"Is that the way it sounds?"

"Pretty much," he said.

"Well, look at it this way. I didn't hold a gun on you at the beginning and I'm not holding a gun on you now. When you're ready to go, you'll go. You know that and so do I."

"I didn't say anything about *going* anyplace."

"I know you didn't. *I* did. I just figure you owe it to yourself to find out where you stand. Once and for all. And maybe you owe it to me too."

Chet sat silent for a long time. Then he said, "When I was going to college, I had a girl friend from Wheeling. Nice girl. Good family. Her name was Doris. We were talking about getting married. Then one day it hit me. Her mouth looked just like Jossie's. At a distance, when you saw her walking, it looked exactly like Jossie's walk. I never felt right about Doris after that. I felt like I was cheating her some way."

"What happened?"

"We broke up. I left school not long after that and
. . . well, that was it."

Sarah got up, walked to the table by the window, and
poured herself a drink. When she sat down again she
said, "I think you'd better take my advice. Go up to West
Virginia and get yourself squared away."

22

They kept to themselves, long days in the woods, walking, shooting, swimming, Chet and Kermit alone sometimes, Kermit and Jossie alone, or the three of them,
food and beer in a basket, eating in the shade under the
trees, sleeping on soft moss, gathering wildflowers for
the house along steep trails.

And long evenings at home, hours at supper around
the kitchen table. Or tilted back in chairs outside, creaking in the porch swing or rocking in the oak rockers.
When the food was low, when the bourbon bottle went
dry, or the beer ran out, someone, usually Chet, went
into Kittredge for supplies. But mostly they kept to
themselves.

At last, however, far along in the second week, Jossie
went into town with Chet. As she came out of the store
carrying two sacks of groceries, she met her mother.

"I heard you were still here," Clara said, "but you
couldn't prove it by me. I haven't seen you in over a
week."

"No, I guess not." Jossie kept walking toward the
parked motorcycle. Clara fell into step beside her.

"Makes a person feel like a damned fool when
you don't even show your face from one week to the
next."

"I haven't been down in town."

"People ask me what you're up to and I don't know what to say."

"Tell them you haven't seen me. Tell them the truth."

"I do. But they look at me like I'm crazy. It's not natural when a daughter never works it out to stop by for a cup of coffee or a glass of beer . . ."

"It's like I said, Mom."

". . . or to sit down and talk a little."

"I've been busy. I really have." She lowered the bags of groceries into the sidecar.

"Come over now," Clara said. "We'll sit on the porch together so people can see . . . you know what I mean."

"I can't, Mom. I have to round up Chet and get on back to the house."

Her mother stood looking at her, squinting in the sunlight, her lips trembling. Finally she said, "You're making an ass of yourself. Don't you know that? Doesn't it matter to you? People making fun of you. Whispering about you living up there with two men the way you are."

"I'm just living with one of them. Everybody knows that."

"Maybe they do and maybe they don't. All I know is I'm so ashamed I don't know what to say to people."

"Don't say anything."

Clara's chin began to quiver then and two great tears squeezed free and ran down her cheeks. "Oh God," she said. "God help us."

"What's the matter?"

"I'm just glad your dad's not here to see what's going on."

"So am I," Jossie said

23

"In answer to a flood of requests," Chet said, "mostly from divorce lawyers and undertakers, I would like to sing a sentimental number."

It was late afternoon, the sun slanting orange between the trees, deep shadows striping across the forest floor. Jossie and Kermit sat on a blanket by the creek edge and Chet stood just in front of them, one foot up on a stump, his guitar resting across his thigh.

He started to sing, husky-voiced, conversational.

> Once I had a girlie,
> But she didn't treat me right,
> So I put her on the griddle,
> And she sizzled all the night.
> That's how I am, I'm sentimental.
> Once I had a honey,
> Who was pretty as a doll,
> But she wouldn't stay at home,
> So I nailed her to the wall.
> That's how I am, I'm sentimental.
> Once I had a baby,
> But she liked to slip around,
> So I locked her in a box,
> And I kept her underground.
> That's how I am, I'm sentimental.

Jossie picked up a clod of dirt and tossed it at Chet. "What kind of a song do you call that?"

Chet leaned his guitar carefully against a tree. "It's a love song," he said. He spun around in a tight circle, crossed his eyes, ran to the creek edge and dived in with his clothes on. Jossie and Kermit sat watching him. He floated on his back spouting water like a whale and barking like a seal.

"We better not watch him," Kermit said. "Or he'll drown himself. Just for a laugh."

They turned around on the blanket with their backs to the creek.

"What was that fella's name you told me about, the one with the father who owns grocery stores?"

"Torchiana. Marty Torchiana. We've been bunking together ever since they shipped us to Germany. He's a good guy. Never stops laughing."

"You think he meant it about the job? If he laughs so much . . ."

"Sure he meant it. His dad has a whole chain of stores, all over Georgia and Florida."

"Do you think you'd like that kind of a job?"

"I guess so," Kermit said. "It's clean work, regular hours, and the wages are pretty good. Besides that, you get your groceries for next to nothing."

"That's what my brother says. He's been with the Dixon Foods people for almost three years. Over at Huntington."

"All we'd have to spend is whatever it costs for an apartment. We could look for one close to the store so I wouldn't have to lay out bus fare. Or maybe we could even find a little house to rent."

"Wouldn't that be nice? I wish we could do it now."

An hour later, the sun out of sight behind the west ridge, the air sharply cooler, they stood in a dark grove of spruce, Chet with his back against a tree, the clothes still heavy and damp on his body, Kermit and Jossie, side by side, facing him.

"All right, I'll make this short," Chet said. "I know you've both made your minds up. Otherwise you wouldn't be standing here like a couple of nitwits. And I know there's nobody around who objects. So I figure we can move right ahead. The main thing is that you both like each other. I mean you get along pretty well together and neither one of you is out to make the other one miserable. So if nobody can think of anything I left out . . . in sickness and health, till death do us part, and all that crap . . . I now pronounce you man and wife." He touched Kermit on the shoulder and said, "That's your cue, dead-ass. Kiss the bride so we can head back to the house and have a drink."

They walked slowly home through the twilight woods, Chet still talking. "I never understood why you have to be married by a stranger. I mean what's so great about kneeling down on a hard floor in front of some lunatic you never saw before. Seems to me people should get married at home, by a good friend, have a few drinks and some food, fall into bed, and do some serious consummating."

24

Late that night, the forest deep and still outside, Jossie lay on her side looking at Kermit.

"Are you awake?" she said.

"Not quite. How about you?"

"I was just lying here thinking."

"What about?"

"You think that's what Chet meant by 'serious consummating'?"

"Seemed pretty serious to me. Nobody laughed."

She moved closer to him and rested her head in the hollow of his shoulder. "I love it when we talk about having a place where we can live together."

"We'll have it. Don't worry about it."

"I can't wait." She raised up on her elbow, looked down at him, and said, "Can we do something crazy?"

"Sure. Why not?"

"It's nothing important. It's just . . . can we go down and sit on the front porch?"

"Now?"

"You don't want to, do you?"

"You know what time it is?" Kermit said.

"About three in the morning, I guess."

"And you want to sit on the porch?"

"I told you it was crazy."

"No, it's not. Let's go."

He got up, put on his shorts and a shirt and they went downstairs, Jossie in her nightgown, and sat in two rockers, side by side, with their feet up on the railing. After a long silent time, she said, "Two more nights." When he didn't answer, she said, "I know we promised not to count, but I can't help it."

"That's all right."

"I'm gonna die when you get on that bus."

"No, you're not. You're too ugly to die."

"You think there's a chance they'll station you someplace here in this country?"

"Sure there is. That's what I aim to ask for."

"If they do, I could come there, couldn't I?" She got up, moved over, and sat down on his lap.

"I guess so," he said. "If I couldn't find anybody better."

"There *ain't* anybody better."

"Pretty sure of yourself, aren't you?"

"When I'm sitting here like this, I am." She put her hands on either side of his face and kissed him. For a long time. When she pulled her mouth away she whispered, "Do it to me."

"You want to go back upstairs?"

"No. Right here. Please." She stood up quickly and pulled her gown off over her head.

"You'll drive the raccoons crazy," he said.

"I don't care." She sat down on his lap again, facing

him, her legs over the arms of the rocking chair. "Oh Jesus," she said, "I'm dying."

"You want to rock a little?"

"Yes," she whispered, her mouth close to his ear. "Yes, honey . . . that's what . . . that's what I . . . oh, God, Kermit . . ."

She collapsed against him with her arms around his neck, and the chair kept rocking gently back and forth, making a soft creaking sound in the dark.

25

Chet leaned over a high stump, hammering an empty beer can with a smooth rock. Concentrated as a silversmith, he pounded and crushed the thin metal into a flat, irregular shape. Holding the disk in his right hand, he walked to the center of a clearing, eighty yards due south of the house. Kermit stood there waiting, holding a cocked shotgun easy in front of him.

"You all set?" Chet said.

"Let her rip."

Chet bent double, his arm down, the metal disk touching the ground. Then he straightened up suddenly, his arm came around like a whip, and the flat piece of metal sailed high in the air, true and straight, almost as high as the trees that bordered the clearing. At the peak of its arc, Kermit brought the shotgun up, sighted, and blasted. The disk shattered. Shreds and strips of metal showered down on the ground.

"You're five up, you bastard," Chet said.

"You didn't plan to beat me, did you?"

"I'm still trying."

"You been trying for fifteen years." Kermit put his hand in his jacket pocket and came up empty. "I'm out of shells."

"That's a cheap way to win," Chet said.

"We can finish up with a rifle if you want to."

"I can't beat you with a rifle either."

"First time I heard you admit it."

"I can out-rassle you . . ." Chet said.

"Wrong."

". . . out-run you . . ."

"Wrong."

". . . out-drink you . . ."

"Wrong."

". . . but I can't out-shoot you."

"Right."

They heard a shrill whistle from the house. Through the trees, they saw Jossie on the porch in an apron, waving a dish towel over her head.

"I guess it's time to eat," Kermit said.

"That's what my stomach says."

When they came inside through the kitchen door, Jossie said, "I've got a surprise for you. At least I think I have."

"What's that?" Kermit said.

"Maybe she cooked a decent meal for a change," Chet said.

"See that flour-can over on the sideboard," Jossie said. "Look inside of it."

Kermit walked to the sideboard and picked up the can. He took the lid off, reached inside and pulled out a brown envelope. He looked at Jossie. "I give up. What is it?"

"I don't know," she said. "I didn't open it."

Kermit tore the envelope open and took out a thin packet of papers, held together by a rubberband.

"What is it?" Jossie said.

"A bunch of money orders I sent home from Germany. She never cashed them it looks like. Must be six or seven hundred dollars here."

"Some party we could have with that," Chet said. "Nothing but Jack Daniels and pecan pie for ten days."

"No, we don't," Jossie said. "Kermit's got something else to spend that money on."

26

The sign over the gate said: ALVIS BEECH—MONUMENTS AND GRAVESTONES. Inside the wire fence, three strands of barbed wire at the top of it, an open shed at one end of the lot, benches and pulleys and power tools, racks of mallets, stone hammers, and chisels against one wall. And scattered around the area blocks of limestone and granite, some fresh from the quarry, some half-shaped, others finished and polished, names and dates chiseled into their smooth surfaces.

Alvis Beech, sixty years old, thin as wire, leather skin gray with stone dust, arms corded and muscled, prominent bulging veins, one finger missing from his left hand, blue overalls patched at the knees, goggles pushed up into a shock of coarse white hair, stood at the center of his property, one hand stroking the top of a four-foot block of red granite, Kermit and Jossie and Chet facing him.

"I ought to get more for it. It's not local stone. You can tell that. I had it trucked down from Vermont."

"I want the best I can get for the money," Kermit said, "but all I got is six hundred. So if it's not this piece, it'll have to be something else."

"Well, you suit yourself. No question but what I can give you a nice piece of limestone for six hundred."

Kermit and Chet exchanged a look. Then Chet turned to Mr. Beech and said, "Walk over here with me for just a minute, sir. I want to ask you a question or two." He took Beech by the elbow and steered him a good distance away from Kermit and Jossie. "Here's the situation, Mr. Beech. We've got a member of the U.S. Army here, a man who's serving his country over in Europe. His mother passed on suddenly and he's back here for a few days to get hold of a nice tombstone for her grave. You see what I mean? It's not your regular buying-and-selling situation."

"It is with me. Buying and selling. That's what I do."

"What I'm saying is there's other things to consider," Chet said.

"I guess you're driving at something, but I don't know what it is. Most of my customers are people who just had somebody die in their family. That don't entitle them to any special treatment or discount rates."

"I see," Chet said. "All right, let's look at it another way. A business like this, I'll bet you like to get paid in cash whenever you can. Is that right?"

Mr. Beech nodded his head. "Cash money. I got the signs up all over. I've got no time or patience for all that paperwork and checks that come back from the bank."

"I can't blame you," Chet said. "Now, I just have one other thing to say. I got an uncle named Hugh Mobley, my dad's kid brother, and he's head of the whole Internal Revenue office up at Wheeling. Those are the Federal income tax people, you know. What they do is snoop around. That's what they get paid for. Just about all they're good for is to poke into other people's business. You know what I mean?"

Mr. Beech didn't answer, but a soft change passed over his face.

"Here's my proposition, Mr. Beech. Either you sell that fine piece of granite to my friend for a proper serviceman's discount of, say, four hundred dollars or I will pick up that telephone over there and call my Uncle Hugh up in Wheeling. Once I do that, I promise you, all hell is sure to break loose. Tomorrow morning there will be two hard-nosed accountants paying you a visit. Going over every sales slip, invoice, shipping order, telephone bill, and love letter that's come through this gate in the last twenty years. You understand what I'm talking about, Mr. Beech?"

Mr. Beech understood. His eyes hooded over, he jammed his hands deep into his pants pockets, and squirted a stream of tobacco juice into the dust at his feet. After a long moment he said, "Fifteen minutes ago I'd never laid eyes on you. Now all of a sudden you're threatening to get the government people after me. Who the hell are you, anyway?"

"I'm your fairy godmother. Looking after your best interests."

27

At a self-service Mobil station four miles south of Dunstan, Chet was hosing gas into the motorcycle, Kermit standing beside him, Jossie in the sidecar. Chet was laughing.

"I still don't know what you told him," Kermit said.

"Never mind. I got the job done, didn't I?"

"Come on, Chet," Jossie said. "What did you say?"

Chet pulled the nozzle out of the tank and hung it back on the pump. "Simple little story," he said. "I told him you were a mutilated soldier with four or five Purple Hearts, that your daddy blew up in a mine accident and your mom got clawed to death by a tiger in the zoo at Richmond."

"Mutilated? Why'd you tell him that? He could look at me and see I wasn't mutilated."

"Not the way I described it. I told him you had a heart transplant, a plastic kidney, an aluminum kneecap, a steel plate in your head, and a rubber dick. If

I'd had five more minutes with him, he'd have handed you that tombstone as a present. Might even have paid you to take it off his hands."

"You crazy bastard."

"I'm not crazy. I'm protecting my Jack Daniels."

"I wish he could have had it ready quicker," Jossie said. "With your mom's name chiseled on it and everything."

"He said a week. Ten days at the outside," Chet said. "That's pretty fast."

"I mean it would have been nice if Kermit could be here when they put the stone on the grave."

"Well, maybe I will be."

"How you figure that?" Chet said. "You're due to head back tomorrow."

"That's right. I'm supposed to. But the way I look at it, these are special circumstances. I guess the army can wait for a few more days."

"Won't you get in trouble?" Jossie said.

"A little, maybe. But not much. Guys show up late all the time. There's a million excuses you can give."

"Like what?"

"I'll just tell the truth. I'll tell them my mother died."

"That was a couple months ago."

"I won't tell them *that.*"

28

For the next week, Chet and Kermit worked every day in the burial plot. They tore down what was left of the old fence, dug new post holes and set in cedar posts. Then they strung woven wire, five feet high, tight around the enclosure, two strands of barbed wire at the top and three-foot-high chicken wire at the bottom to keep the ground squirrels out.

When the fence was finished, they weeded and spaded and raked inside, over the graves and around them, laid new drainage tile, sowed grass seed, and scattered fertilizer on top of it. Finally, they built forms at the head of Mrs. Docker's grave, mixed up a batch of concrete, and poured a solid foundation to support the granite stone when it came.

"You did good work out there," Jossie said, the day after they finished. She was hanging wet clothes on a rope line. Kermit was just next to her, in a hammock stretched between two trees.

"I damn near wore Chet out. He's not used to lifting anything heavier than a shot glass."

"Where'd he go? I haven't seen him since breakfast."

"He's down at Jernegan's, I guess, showing off the blisters on his hands."

Jossie hung up the last piece of laundry, wiped her hands on her apron, and walked over to the hammock.

"Move over."

"Pretty tricky maneuver," Kermit said. "Two people in a hammock."

"I didn't have anything fancy in mind."

"That's different. If you guarantee . . ."

"I don't guarantee anything."

He held the hammock steady while she eased in beside him. She lay on her back with her head on his shoulder. "Not bad," she said, looking up at the foliage, the breeze off the mountains cooling her cheeks, "but not the best place in the world for fooling around."

"You couldn't prove it by me."

"Bull."

"A clean mind in a clean body. That's my style."

"You don't lie any better than you ever did."

"Gargle twice a day, shampoo twice a week, and sleep ten hours every night."

"Sure," she said. "What about those German girls?

You never told me if you like them or not."

"You never asked me."

"I'm asking you now."

"The truth is," Kermit said. "They don't have any girls in Germany. They only keep the boy children."

"Who has the babies then?"

"That's what they build all those factories for. You've seen the pictures. Everything clean and scientific."

"Chet bet me you had at least twenty girls over there."

"The first week I did. After that I tapered off."

"Well . . . I don't care," Jossie said.

"Course not."

"I'd hate to be some kind of a watchdog. Peeking around corners to see what a man's up to."

"That's a pretty grown-up attitude. Is that the way I'm supposed to feel too?"

"It's different for you. You *know* what I've been doing. Working in Dunstan, working in McKeesport, pouring coffee and frying eggs."

"You sure you didn't cuddle up with some of those truck drivers hauling oranges up from Florida?"

"Only the fat ones," she said. "When the nights were chilly."

"Makes sense."

"Matter of fact I didn't have anything to do with anybody except the big spenders, the ones that ordered the complete dinner and left a quarter tip."

"It's part of the job, I guess."

"No question about it."

"What about that state cop? The one who chauffeured you up here the other day. What's his name?"

"Jim August. He's so stuck on himself he doesn't need a woman."

"I don't know. He looks like a contender to me."

"Not in my book. I wouldn't pee on him if he caught fire."

29

The truck drove down from Dunstan on a Saturday, the tombstone in the back, wrapped up in canvas. The driver and his helper unloaded it and positioned it on the foundation at the head of the grave.

The next day after church, Melvin and Agnes brought the children up. They picked wildflowers, tied them in bunches and laid them at the foot of the monument. And Melvin read from the Bible.

Agnes and Jossie brought out platters of fried chicken, bowls of potato salad, bean salad, and deviled eggs. Hot rolls, pitchers of lemonade, and a blueberry pie. They ate and talked, sitting on the grass in the shade, and later when the women were carrying dishes inside, Chet and Kermit played catch with Melvin and his oldest boy, Wayne, age eight.

"Old Wayne's got an arm on him, Melvin."

"Yeah. I reckon he'll be a man before his mother is."

"I mean it. He's really got some steam on it."

"He'll be up there in Pittsburgh next thing you know," Kermit said. "Pitching for the Pirates. You and Agnes'll be sitting in box seats, drinking beer, all puffed up like peacocks."

"That'll be the day," Melvin said.

"Bound to happen. He's got a hummer there."

"Keep smoking it, Wayne. You'll have your dad rubbing his hand before long."

At the sink inside the house, Agnes and Jossie watched the men through the kitchen windows.

"I hope Kermit don't get in any trouble," Agnes said.

"He's going back tomorrow."

"I know that's what he says. But even so he's a week or ten days late."

"He's not worried about it," Jossie said.

"Course not. He don't worry about anything. Never has. He's lucky and he knows it. Born lucky, I guess. Mom used to say, 'You got the looks in the family, Aggie, but Kermit got the luck!' Mom knew. She could tell a lot just by looking at people."

"I read someplace that if you think you're lucky, you'll be lucky."

"I don't know about that," Agnes said. "Melvin talks about luck all the time, but he never seems to have any."

"That's cause he always talks about *bad* luck."

"That's right. You hit the nail on the head there." She pulled the curtain aside. "Look at Wayne out there, all red-faced, thinking he's a man already. He'll wear himself out before he's through."

Late in the afternoon, when Melvin and Agnes had gone home and Chet was down at Jernegan's, Kermit and Jossie walked out to the graves and looked across the fence at the red granite monument.

"It looks fine, Kermit."

"Yeah, it does. He did a good job of it."

30

Mid-morning the next day, a new Chevrolet sedan, painted olive drab, U.S. ARMY stencilled on both front doors, sat in the shade across the street from Jernegan's store, a young military policeman behind the wheel; Dale Roach, born in Great Falls, Montana, twenty-eight years old, ten of those years spent in the army.

The door to the grocery store opened and closed and another military policeman crossed the street to the car, Joe Meeker, forty-one, thick-set and husky, nose broken, a scar over one eye, veteran of a hundred street fights, service ribbons from Japan, Korea, and Vietnam pinned to his tunic.

"Any luck?" Roach said.

"Can't pee a drop with these people. I might as well be talking Chinese."

"My dad told me if you want information be sure you don't go to a red-neck."

"He told the truth, it looks like."

Down the street, Clara Floyd angled across her yard and headed toward Jernegan's.

"Here comes a new face," Roach said.

"You think it's worth a shot?"

"Why not?" He got out of the car and the two of them eased across the street to intercept Clara. Meeker gave her a soft salute and said, "Excuse me, ma'am. We're here on army business. Trying to locate a family name of Docker."

Clara's eyes wavered, then came up in a look as direct as she could manage. "I don't know a soul by that name."

"It's a soldier named Kermit Docker," Roach said. "His pedigree says he came from here."

"I still don't know him."

"You lived here long?" Meeker said.

"All my life, off and on."

"And there's no Docker family around here?"

"Not that I know of."

They watched her as she moved around them and walked on to the store. As she stepped up to the porch, a car turned into the street behind her. It crawled forward, stopped behind the army car, and Jim August got out.

31

Kermit sat on a chair near the kitchen window, in underpants and his army shirt, cleaning and oiling his shotgun. Jossie, just beside him, was pressing his pants on a fold-up ironing board. Chet, in an apron, a beer can in one hand, a skillet in the other, was busy at the stove.

"I shouldn't do this to you, Kermit. It's not fair for me to break things up between you and Jossie. But I don't know how to keep from it. Once you taste my cooking, you'll tie a tin can to her tail. No question about it."

"Sure is noisy in here," Jossie said.

"Any chef will tell you, it's the *touch* that counts," Chet went on. "When you first pick an egg up in your hand, that egg can *tell,* before you crack it, if you know what you're doing."

"You ever heard such crap in your life?" Kermit said to Jossie.

"Not since he went to sleep last night." She handed Kermit his pants, took his army blouse off the back of a chair and put it on a wire hanger.

"Same thing with a slice of bacon," Chet said. "Once that cutting knife bites in, it's all decided."

Jossie walked toward the windows, carrying the hanger. She hung it on a wall peg near where Kermit was sitting.

"Put on your pants before they get wrinkled."

"Yeah, I will. I'm almost done here."

Chet waved the butcher knife over his head. "If you just hack away at a side of bacon, one slice thick and the next one thin as paper . . ."

Jossie looked out the window as the army car rolled to a stop at the head of the lane. Roach got out on one side,

Meeker on the other. Jossie pulled back behind the curtain. "Shhh." Chet stopped talking. Kermit looked up. "Two soldiers just drove up out front," she said.

Kermit moved to the side of the window. Roach and Meeker were standing by their car, talking and examining the house.

"Looks like I'll get a free ride back to Camp Lee," Kermit said. He picked up his pants and started to put them on.

"Does that mean they're here to arrest you?"

"No. Nothing like that. They just came to escort me back to the post. They do it for all us important non-coms."

"Cut it out. Tell me the truth."

"All right. The truth is they might give me latrine duty and restrict me to the base for a while. But that's all. It'll blow over." He started toward the door. "Warm the coffee up and I'll invite them in."

Chet put a hand on his arm. "Wait a minute. Don't go out yet. Let me have a little fun with them first."

"What kind of fun?"

"I'll go out there and kid around a little and they'll think I'm you. We'll get some laughs."

Roach and Meeker were halfway between their car and the house when Chet came out on the porch, still wearing an apron, carrying a wooden spoon in his hand.

"Looks like we flushed one out," Roach said.

"One what?" Meeker said.

Chet came down off the porch and walked toward them. "Morning," he said. "What can I do for you?"

Meeker said they were looking for the Docker place. "You found it."

"We wanted to talk to a man named Docker."

"I guess you mean Kermit."

"That's right," Roach said. "Is he here?"

"Not exactly." Chet nodded his head in the direction of the family graveyard. "You see, Kermit had a little bad luck."

"What kind of bad luck?"

"We buried him last Thursday."

Behind the curtains at the kitchen window, Kermit and Jossie looked out.

"What do you suppose he's saying?" Jossie said.

"God knows. Some cock-and-bull story."

Outside, Meeker said, "How'd it happen?"

"Just a freak accident as far as anybody could tell. Seems like he was climbing over a fence, carrying his shotgun, and he accidentally shot himself. Then when he fell he cut his throat on the barbed wire. After that, he rolled down the bluff into the creek and drowned."

Roach walked across the barn lot to the graveyard, studied the new grave for a moment, then came back.

"According to the headstone, that's where his mother is buried."

"That's right," Chet said. "She keeled over from grief when she heard about Kermit. So we put the two of them in the casket together. That's a custom around here. Sort of like going back to the womb."

Roach and Meeker exchanged a look. Then Meeker said to Chet, "Is your name Docker, too?"

"No. My name's McKinley. William McKinley."

"You ever been in the service, Mr. McKinley?"

"No. I tried to enlist but they wouldn't have me."

"How's that?" Roach said.

"I never sorted it out," Chet said, a serious expression on his face. "Unless maybe it was the clothes I had on. You see, my folks were dirt-poor when I was a kid. So the only clothes I ever got were hand-me-downs. That would have been all right, I guess, except the rest of the kids in my family were girls. So I wore dresses and skirts all the time I was growing up. I got used to dressing that way and folks around here got used to it too. I mean nobody ever noticed me much till I went for my army physical."

"You mean you showed up for your physical wearing your sister's clothes?"

"No, I didn't," Chet said. "Not *that* day. For once I had a brand new outfit. My mother and the girls spent over a week making it. It was kind of a powder-blue suit with a short jacket and a pleated skirt. And they took one of Mom's old hats and made it over. Sewed a lot of paper flowers on it. Then Hulda, that's my oldest sister, let me use her white shoes. And the pocketbook she carried the day she got married. I didn't have any silk stockings but everybody said I looked all right anyway."

Inside, Jossie said, "What do you think they're talking about for so long?"

"Chet will give you a run-down later. You can count on that."

Meeker studied Chet's face carefully. "And you say the army turned you down?"

Chet nodded. "I felt awful about it. They didn't even check my pulse. A man just asked me some questions and they sent me home."

"I'll tell you what," Roach said. "Why don't you ride into Elkins with us and see if maybe we can't get this whole thing straightened out."

"I don't think I could do that. I'm pretty busy right now."

"It won't take more than a few minutes. Tell you the truth, it wouldn't surprise me if your name turned out to be Docker."

"No. You got it wrong," Chet said, glancing back toward the house. "This is the Docker house, like I said, but I'm Jack Pershing."

"I thought you said McKinley."

"That's right," Chet said. "William McKinley."

Roach stepped up close to Chet. "Cut the shit, kid. We

heard enough jack-off stories to last us a while. Let's go find out what the truth is." He reached out and took hold of Chet's upper arm.

Chet shook him off and twisted away. "Now wait a minute. Don't start grabbing at anybody."

Roach grabbed him again, both hands this time, and Meeker moved in, his hand gripping the handle of his night stick.

Chet twisted free again. He dropped the wooden spoon and shoved Roach back with both hands. "I told you . . . keep your hooks off of me." He turned quickly, then ducked under the swing of Meeker's night stick. Crouching low, he got a foot behind Meeker's ankle, then shoved him hard in the chest. Meeker sprawled on his back in the dirt. As Chet turned back, Roach swung his night stick and caught him just behind the ear.

As Chet fell face down, Roach raised the club again. But a shotgun roared ten feet behind him and dirt and gravel sprayed against his legs as the blast ripped into the ground at his feet. When he turned around he saw Kermit, the gun leveled, Jossie standing a few feet behind him.

"All right," Kermit said. "Let's stop everything right there. Put your hands on your heads, both of you, and walk over here to me."

As Kermit took their holster guns and tossed them on the grass behind him, Jossie knelt down by Chet.

"How's he look?" Kermit said.

"There's not much blood. But he's awful white."

"We'd better get him to the hospital. Back their car over here and we'll load him in it."

As she ran to the car, Kermit stepped back and gestured with the shotgun. "All right now, nice and easy. You two march yourselves around to the back of the house. And stay close together. If I have to shoot you, I want to be sure I hit you both with one shell."

32

Kermit came out through the main entrance of the Elkins hospital, down the steps, and across the parking lot. He opened the door of the army car and slid in under the wheel. Jossie was waiting in the front seat.

"What did the doctor say?"

"Not much of anything. Chet's got a big knot on his head and he'll need a few stitches, I guess, but he doesn't look as white as he did."

"Is there anything we can do?"

"Not right now. They've got him doped up. The doctor says he won't be talking much till tomorrow."

He started the car, pulled out of the parking lot, and turned right toward the south-bound highway.

"We going back to the house?" Jossie said.

"We have to. I don't want to get busted for stealing an army car."

"What happens when we get there?"

"I don't know. We'll have to wait and see."

"Those guys are going to be pretty sore at you."

"I wouldn't be surprised."

"What do you think they'll do?"

"I don't know. Arrest me, I guess. Take me over to Camp Lee."

"Then what?"

"Well, that depends on what they decide to throw at me."

She turned in the seat then, looked out the window so he couldn't see her face. "You're not fooling anybody," he said. "I can tell when you're crying."

"I can't help it."

"You won't change anything by doing that."

"I don't care. I can't help it. I'm scared."

"There's nothing to be scared of."

"I know. That's what you always say. But I feel like the sand is running right out of me. Just this morning we had everything going our way. I didn't even feel rotten about you going back because I knew we had a lot of good stuff to look forward to. Now, all of a sudden, it's just . . . I don't know . . . it's like we're never supposed to have anything good. Nothing for ourselves. Nothing to hope for."

They sat silent then, the rest of the way down to Beverly, Jossie looking out the window, Kermit's eyes straight ahead, his jaw muscles hard under the skin.

Just below Beverly, after the Kittredge turn-off, he angled left on a dirt road that circles north around Kittredge.

"Where we going?" Jossie said.

"I want you to do something for me. Will you do it?"

"Course I will. If I can."

"You can do it."

"I'm just scared."

"There's nothing to be scared of. I already told you that."

The car moved along the narrow road, abandoned houses and barns, gray and dilapidated, off through the trees. But no people, no cars, no dogs barking.

At last they turned off on a rutted, over-grown logging road. Kermit followed it for three-quarters of a mile, maneuvering slowly through fallen limbs and tangles of weeds and bush, till he came to a clearing. He turned the car around and got out. Jossie slid under the wheel and drove back down the road. Kermit watched till the car was out of sight. Then he turned and walked away through the trees.

33

Roach and Meeker sat back-to-back on opposite sides of a young hickory tree, their hands behind them, cuffed together, their linked arms encircling the tree trunk.

"How long we been here?" Roach said.

"Damned if I know. Two hours, I guess."

"I have to piss so bad my back teeth are floating."

"You'd better get used to it. We could be in for a long sit."

"I still don't know how that bastard got the drop on us. We should have jumped him."

"If you had, you wouldn't need to take a leak right now. You'd be cold and stiff with a hundred little holes in your belly."

"He couldn't have got both of us."

"Why not? These ridge-runners cut their teeth on a gun muzzle. He'd just as soon shoot you as look at you. And he might do it yet."

"Not a chance. He's long gone."

"Don't be too sure of that. I'd say it depends on what happens to that buddy of his. How hard did you hit him?"

"Hard enough to drop him. I don't know . . ."

They heard the car engine then. It gunned to top the rise at the end of the lane, idled, then cut off. The car door opened, slammed shut, and a moment later Jossie came around the corner of the house. She stood looking down at the two men. "Where did he leave the keys to those cuffs?"

"Up there on the porch," Roach said.

Jossie crossed over to the back porch, picked up a key case lying by the door, came back and unlocked the handcuffs. Roach jumped to his feet as soon as he was free, clutching at the front of his pants. He ran a few steps, then stopped, his back turned to Jossie.

"What's the matter with him?" she said to Meeker just before the water began to splash against the ground. "Oh, I see," she said.

"Where's Docker?" Meeker said, rubbing his wrists.

"Your guns are inside on the kitchen table and your car's out in front with the keys in it."

"God damn it, I asked you where Docker was."

"Listen, don't mouth off at me. I'm not in the army. I'm the one who just unlocked you. Remember?"

"Yeah, but . . ."

"But nothing. I could have forgotten you were here. This is no crossroads, you know. You could have sat here till the ground-squirrels made a nest in your underwear."

"Yeah, all right. You're right."

"That's better. We took Chet to the Miners' Infirmary in Dunstan. Kermit's up there with him. He's waiting for you."

She followed the two men as they hurried around the house. She watched them get in the car, turn around, and drive down the lane toward Kittredge. Then she ran into the house.

34

Sitting in the shade, his back against a tree, Kermit dug in the dead leaves with one hand and came up with a walnut. He balanced it on the side of his forefinger like a marble, then flipped it away in a high arc with his thumb.

Thirty feet away, a gray squirrel zigzagged down a tree trunk and ran nervous, stop-and-go, to the nut. Eyes on

Kermit, he picked it up and held it between his front paws, balancing himself on his haunches. Frozen motion, he sat there, till a noise, behind him to his left, startled him. He popped the walnut into his mouth and vanished up the blind side of the tree trunk.

Kermit, too, was up quickly and out of sight. He stayed hidden till Jossie, wearing denim jeans, a shirt, and a man's sweater, came up the logging road to the clearing, trundling the motorcycle beside her.

"You made good time," Kermit said.

"I hurried as fast as I could."

"What about the M.P.'s?"

"I sent them to Dunstan."

"Good for you." He leaned over the sidecar, poked through the blanket rolls and camp gear she'd put there. "Did you bring everything?"

"I think so."

Kermit pulled out a roll of burlap, something heavy and firm in the center of it. "What's this?"

"Your shotgun. I didn't think you'd want to go off without it."

"I guess you're right. I might as well take it."

He pushed the motorcycle to the far side of the clearing, Jossie walking beside him. "You all set?" he said.

"I guess so. I haven't had time to think."

"Good. "You're better off that way. You're not gonna cry anymore, are you?"

"Not if I can help it. I'm no cry-baby. You know that. I never was."

"You were doing pretty good a while ago," he said.

"It wasn't for myself. I was worrying over you. I just hate the idea of people chasing you."

"Don't worry. They won't chase me long. I'm not a big enough cheese."

Part Three

35

In the meanest days of the nineteen thirties, a group of jobless writers, under government subsidy, produced a series of books describing in detail every square mile of this country, every city and village, every county and township, mountain, stream, and valley. Every cranny. Every corner.

The area around Kittredge was carefully pictured.

Over the extensive flat of broken and jumbled sandstone on the mountain plays a hard, whipping breeze, crisp and chill even in mid-summer. The northern face of the mountain, which fires have stripped of trees, is thickly covered with bracken, great willow herb, mosses, chokeberry, fetid currant, and wild bleeding heart. Wintergreen, trailing arbutus, mountain cranberry and holly, red raspberry, pink moccasin flower and the round-leafed orchid are common.

The western slope is more thickly wooded with ground and running pine, mountain ash, and maple and laurel, red spruce, wild cherry, and yellow birch. Along the source of Red Lick Run and in other moist corners grows the deep-rooted, bright-green American hellebore.

Below and on all sides is a panorama of the most mountainous section of a mountain state, a section buckled and folded by prehistoric upheavals of earth, gouged by racing streams for centuries. East and south the steep crests roll to the horizons in long parallel waves, the Shenandoah mountains billowing above the rest. Lower crests to the north and west, massed between the long chains of Allegheny, Rich, Cheat, and Shavers mountains, some covered with unbroken forest, some scarred by fire and erosion . . .

Rough and tangled, unchanged from its description forty years before, this hard country folded around Kermit and Jossie. They disappeared on its empty trails that uncertain afternoon, running away.

36

"Which way are we heading?" Jossie said.

They were still on the logging road, pushing the motorcycle.

"Due east right now. I'm pointing for the tow path on Shavers Fork. When we hit that we'll ride the sickle south till we're just west of Valley Head. I figure we'll cut through to the Clover Lick road and then south and west till we get to Bluefield."

"How long will it take us?"

"I don't know. And I don't care much. We'll just hit an easy clip and stay out of sight. That's the main thing. We'll get there when we get there."

So they took their time, down the tow road, through the woods, on service roads, lumber trails, strips of tarvy, packed dirt and gravel, through craggy mountains and thick forest, land as old and unmarked as any they would ever see, home for the black bear still, for the raccoon, mink, and skunk, the possum, woodchuck, and the fox. Quail in the underbrush, grouse, plover, and woodcock. Geese and blue heron by the water, the hawk, the buzzard, and the eagle soaring high. Brook trout in the streams, bass and wall-eyed pike, catfish, bluegill, perch, and suckers. And forest flowers—rhododendron, laurel, hawthorn, redbud, and dogwood, the azalea, yellow and orange, and wild orchids clinging to black tree trunks.

They traveled from dawn to mid-morning most days, from six in the evening till full dark, staying out of sight. Sleeping in some cool pocket of the forest, hunting, fishing, cooking, and eating, making love in the full light and heat of August late-mornings, in gullies, under an overhang of rock, in a sheltered thicket of flowers and berry vines, swimming and laughing, filling in the spaces of the years they'd been apart, and moving steadily southwest, past Cheat Bridge and Valley Head as planned, then east to the road that parallels the old C. and O. lines and the Greenbrier River, down through Cass and Clover Lick to Edray, a fast and short night run on Highway 219 to below Mill Point, then back to quiet roads again, through Denmar, west to Friar's Hill, south through Williamsburg to Alta, then Highway 12, at night again, down through Alderson to Pence Springs, south through Wayside and Greenville to Rock Camp and from there due west and a little south, the fastest leg of the trip, forty-seven miles into Bluefield, two hundred and seventeen crow-flight miles in sixteen days.

37

"What if we can't locate your dad?" Jossie said. It was the morning after they'd started south.

"We'll find him."

"What if we just crossed over into Virginia and kept

going? Wouldn't that be better?"

"Why do you think that?"

"I just thought if they're looking for you, the first place they'd check would be wherever your dad is."

"You talk like there's a big manhunt going on."

"Well, we're not traveling the back roads for nothing. You must have some reason for it."

"I do. You're right. I guess they will go through the motions of looking for me. So I'm not about to run up and down the highways on a red motorcycle. But you have to remember, the army won't peter out just because one corporal went AWOL. I mean they can't afford to tie up a lot of men looking for me. I'm too easy to replace."

"I hope you're right."

"I know I'm right. It'll be two weeks before we get to Bluefield. Maybe longer. I'll be yesterday's news. Between now and then there'll be five hundred soldiers that'll turn up missing. There's no reason to make a big stink about me."

"I'd still feel better about it if we steered clear of Bluefield."

"So would I. But I think I ought to see my dad."

"I thought you were mad at him. Isn't that what you told Chet?"

"Not exactly," he said. "I just thought . . . I don't know what I thought. But I know I want to see him before we leave."

"After that where do we go?"

"I don't know. Wherever you want."

"I've never been anyplace except Pennsylvania. We could go up to McKeesport if you want to. At least I've got a job waiting for me there."

"I don't think that's such a good idea."

"Neither do I," she said. "I hate McKeesport." Then, "Is there any place special you want to go?"

"I just want to keep it open. I want to go wherever my

nose points. I mean if we see a place where we want to stop, then we'll stop. Otherwise, we'll keep on moving."

"What happens when we run out of money?" she said.

"Then I'll work and get some more."

38

Their second night away they camped on the west bank of Shavers Fork. Kermit had shot a squirrel, cleaned it, and cooked it on a spit. After they ate, they sat on their spread-out blankets watching the fire die.

"When did you make up your mind you weren't going back?" Jossie said.

"I don't know for sure."

"One minute we were heading for your house and you were going to give yourself up. The next thing I knew, you'd turned your head clear around."

"I don't know what it was," Kermit said. "It just happened. One minute I was thinking one way and the next minute . . . I don't know . . . I saw you crying there in the car . . ."

"I was scared of what they might do to you. That's why I cried."

"I know that." He got up and layered dead branches on the fire till it burned bright again. When he sat down, he said, "The other thing was I kept seeing that bastard unloading on Chet the way he did. Couldn't get that picture out of my head."

"I hope he's going to be all right. I never saw anybody turn so white like that."

"Don't worry about Chet. You can't kill a lunatic."

39

Three days later, the afternoon close and hot in the forest, they swam in the Greenbrier river, made love on the bank in the shade, then rolled into the stream again like otters, laughing, and splashing. When they came out they sprawled naked in the grass and dried themselves in the sun.

"With a little persuasion I might put up a lean-to and stay right here," Kermit said.

"I'd like it. How long could we stay?"

"I don't know. Sixty years ought to do it. Till I've caught all the fish and cleaned out the squirrels."

"You'd get tired of it, I'll bet."

"I don't think so. Why would I?"

"I don't know. I just think you would. It's too perfect. There's nothing to scrap over. A man has to have some kind of a fight on his hands or he gets edgy."

"Who told you that?" he said.

"Nobody. Nobody had to. I've got eyes. I've seen how my dad is. And different men I've worked for. And those truck drivers who stopped in where I worked. They all have some kind of an itch to test themselves, to prove what kind of men they are. How fast they can drive, how much they can drink, how many girls they can screw between Cleveland and Atlanta. Bragging and cussing and fighting among themselves. And all over nothing. Just to give themselves something to do and make themselves feel important. Strutting around, scratching and belching, they have to *prove* something every day. Put those guys in a quiet place like this and they'd go nuts. Nobody to show off for. Nobody to cheat or out-rassle."

"Are you saying I'm like that?"

"Not so much maybe. But you're a man and you've got

some of those man-traits whether you like it or not. I'm not saying that's a bad thing altogether. But it's something that keeps a person from being peaceful, makes them jerky and jumpy if things are going too smooth. You know what I mean? That's why men keep picking up axes and guns and fishing poles. They have to butcher a steer, chop down a tree, cut the balls off a pig, go fight a war, or screw somebody else's wife. It's their nature."

Kermit raised himself up on one elbow and looked down at her. "What you're saying is you don't want to live here by the river with me. Is that it?"

"No, that's *not* it. I'm just saying you'd get tired of it. Or tired of me. One of the two. Some morning I'd wake up and see you throwing rocks in the river and the next thing I knew you'd be gone. A man has to have aggravation. If he *doesn't* have it, he'll go looking for it."

He rolled close to her on the grass. "How about you," he said. "Are you looking for aggravation?"

"Not me. I hate it."

"Too bad. I thought I might aggravate you a little."

"Is *that* what you call it?"

"Why not? What do you call it?"

She put her arms around his neck and pulled his head close to hers. "I don't call it anything."

40

That night they lay in their blankets, a cool breeze coming down off the west ridge and an owl rustling and moaning in a tree over their heads.

"I want you to do something for me," Kermit said.

"What?"

"I want you to tell me about Fred Baines."

"Oh, Jesus, honey . . ."

"What's the matter?"

"Don't ruin everything."

"I'm not. But it's hard for me to get used to the idea of you being married to somebody. I mean I wouldn't recognize him if I met him in the street."

"I *told* you why I did that."

"Wait a minute. I'm not blaming you for anything. All I'm saying is I know *everything* about you, since you were knee-high. Now all of a sudden . . ."

"If the shoe was on the other foot," Jossie said, "the less I knew, the better I'd like it."

"I don't believe that."

"It's the truth."

"No, it's not," Kermit said. "What if I told you I married a German girl right after I went back last summer and we had a set of twins two months ago? What would you say?"

"You're *not* telling me that, are you?"

"No. I said, 'What if?' "

"I guess I'd bawl my eyes out."

"Then what?"

"I don't know," she said.

"Yes, you do. You'd ask me a million questions."

"No, I wouldn't."

"You mean it wouldn't matter to you if the kids were boys or girls or if they had blue eyes or brown eyes?" He struck a match and held it up so he could see her face. "And it wouldn't matter to you if their mother was short and fat, tall and skinny, dark hair or light hair. Are you trying to tell me you wouldn't have any curiosity about her?"

"Okay, you win," Jossie said. "I see what you're talking about." She settled herself beside him, rested her head on his shoulder.

"Fred Baines," she said. "Age thirty-eight. Brown hair, thin on top. Brown eyes. Five-foot-nine. A hundred and seventy pounds. His dad's had a hardware store in

West Newton for forty years. Fred worked there from the time he quit high school. And when his dad died, the store came to him. By then he was married with two kids. A boy, Harold, and a girl, Emily. His wife's name was Polly. They'd known each other since they were little, just like us, and they got along good, I guess. Anyway . . . three years ago they took a vacation and drove up to Maine, all the way up the coast. Nobody knew if they ate something bad or what. But all four of them got terrible cases of hepatitis. And Polly and the little girl died. In the hospital in Portland."

"Jesus, that's awful."

"Fred couldn't get over it. Just him and the boy in the house alone. He didn't know what to do with himself. So all his friends went out of their way to be nice to him. Mom and Dad and I met him at somebody's house a year ago last January. After that, I saw him around different places and we talked to each other a little bit but that was all there was to it. He felt awkward around women. Never really felt at home anyplace except in his store. Anyway, last summer, after I found out you'd re-enlisted, I went back home like a cripple. Right away, Mom started yelling at me and even Dad said I was crazy to wait around for you. They had me so mixed up I didn't know if I was coming or going. Next thing I knew Fred was standing in our front yard one Sunday afternoon asking me to marry him. I knew at the time it was crazy. But I had to get away from Mom or I'd have killed her. And I was trying to get even with you, too. So I told him I'd marry him and before I could change my mind, we did it. I didn't even think about what I was doing to Fred. And by the time I did think about it, it was too late. The damage was done."

"How do you mean?"

"He knew from the first day it wasn't going to pan out. I couldn't stop crying. He kept having the doctor for me, but it wasn't anything a doctor could fix. Or anybody else. I just stayed in bed and kept on crying. In two weeks I lost over ten pounds. Finally the doctor gave me some sleeping pills. From then on I slept around the clock. And I kept losing weight till I looked like I was made out of pipe cleaners. Everybody was worried sick about me. One day Fred came in and sat down on the edge of my bed. He'd brought me some ice cream and it tasted good to me. First food I'd had for days. While I ate it he sat there looking at me. Finally he said, 'We made a mistake. You don't want to be married to me at all, do you?' I couldn't get any words out but he knew the answer just by looking at me. So that was the end of it. When he left the house the next morning, I packed some things in a bag and took the bus down to Dunstan. I wrote him a letter from there telling him how sorry I was, but I never got an answer. Just some papers from a lawyer, a lot of forms to fill out. By October first I had my annulment papers and by Christmas Fred was married again. A widow woman who'd helped out with the boy after his wife and daughter died.''

Jossie sat up, with one end of the blanket tucked around her. "Now you know as much about Fred Baines as I do.''

4I

One early afternoon, sitting by an abandoned quarry in the shade, Jossie said, "Do you think most people get a fair shake? I mean they keep singing about this being the land of the *free*. I don't know any free people. Do you?"

"If you're not in jail and you can work at anything you want and live wherever you take a notion to, that's *free*.''

"No, it's not. Not for me. Why does a person have to work like a dog, for instance? At some job he hates. Just to keep a little food on the table. What's free about *that*?"

"That's the way things are," he said.

"You bet it is. But I don't have to like it."

"You got a better idea?"

"Don't tease me. I'm serious. I may not be educated but I've got eyes and ears. I can see what's going on. You're looking at me funny. You want me to shut up?"

"No."

"You sure?"

"I'm sure."

"The trouble is we've only got one game. King of the Hill, it's called. That's all we're geared for. The top prize. The world's record. A regular person with a regular job starts to feel like a nothing, like he's some kind of number on a chart. Only big shots are important. Politicians and movie stars and millionaires. That's what they teach us. Even if they're whores or crooks. It doesn't matter, just as long as their names get in the paper. What I'm saying is, most of us are out of the race before it starts. I mean, *Jesus,* all of us can't get to the top of the ladder. Lots of us can't even find the bottom rung. But that's no reason why we should hate ourselves. Or feel like we're second-class merchandise."

"*I* don't feel like that," Kermit said.

"Yes, you do. *Inside* you do. That's why you went in the army."

"No, it's not. I enlisted because I needed a job."

"That's right. That's what I'm talking about. And the only job you could get was in the lousy army. Something you hate."

"I never said I hated it."

"You didn't have to."

42

East of Denmar, nine days after they left Kittredge, Kermit's motorcycle, suffering from over-loading, rough roads, and old age, gave out. In the Calvin Price State Forest, at the bottom of a dry creek bed, thirty yards off the service road, Kermit removed part of the engine, worked on it for five hours, then put it all back together again.

"Is it fixed now?" Jossie said.

"It's patched but it's not fixed. It's too old to fix. You know how long I've had this contraption?"

"I can't remember when you *didn't* have it."

"I was twelve when I got it. And my Uncle Howard had it for a few years before that, third-hand from a war surplus lot in Clarksburg. I'll bet this sickle was already fifteen years old when you were born."

"Will it last till we get to Bluefield?"

"I wouldn't bet on it. It's about due to peter out."

"Then what?" Jossie said.

"Then I'll sell it."

"Who'd want it?"

"Anybody. In this state you can sell anything with wheels. They always figure the motor can be fixed. There isn't a half-wit in West Virginia who doesn't think he's a master mechanic."

The next afternoon, just opposite a one-pump filling station on the road west of Spring Creek, the cycle engine coughed and spit, smoked weakly, and gave up.

"Now what?" Jossie said.

"You see the red-faced guy in coveralls watching us from across the road? In ten minutes he'll be the proud owner of a motorcycle."

Jossie waited under a tree while Kermit wheeled across

the tarvy past the gasoline pump, to a patch of shade just outside the garage door.

While the two men talked and spit, a thin woman came out of the house attached to the garage, a baby on her hip and a five-year-old boy bouncing along in front of her. She examined the motorcycle and the boy climbed into the sidecar.

From beginning to end, the sales transaction took just over twenty minutes. At last, Kermit shook hands with the red-faced man and walked back across the road.

"We're rich," he said.

"You mean he bought it?"

"Didn't I tell you he would?"

"How much?" she said.

"Guess."

"If he paid more than twenty, he's bats."

"He's bats."

"Twenty-five?"

"Thirty-five. And I threw in the tool kit."

"I don't believe it."

"Cash money. It was the sidecar that sold him."

They picked up their blanket rolls and started down the road.

"At least that money will get us to Bluefield."

"Bluefield? As soon as we hit Lewisburg, I thought I'd pick up a new Buick and buzz out to California."

"You're crazy."

"All us rich people are crazy."

"If I'd remembered to bring the rest of those money orders we wouldn't be so short."

"Don't worry about it. Nobody can remember everything."

They walked farther west on the black-top, toward the junction with 219. "You didn't mean that about California, did you?"

"Sure," he said. "Why not?"

"I don't know. I just didn't think about us going that far."

"We can do anything we want. We can go to Seattle and get rained on. Or Missoula and get snowed on."

"I'm serious," she said.

"So am I."

"You said something before about Iowa. That sounded good to me."

"Sounds good to me, too. Corn country. Nice people, they say. Square dances and beer on Saturday. Hot dogs and mustard and chocolate-covered kumquats."

"I never saw you so limber. Did that jay-bird back there slip you a drink?"

"No. I just feel good. It's a nice September afternoon. We don't know where we're going but we're on our way. Can't beat that, can you?"

"No, I guess not."

"I think you're right about Iowa," he said. "Iowa sounds like a good bet. Or Nebraska maybe. I'll bet I could get a job on a big farm out there. That's the thing now. Five-section farms. Or a cattle ranch. They still run a lot of cattle in Nebraska. We could settle in and get in touch with Chet. Drag him out there with us."

"What about his wife?"

"Chet's not married. I'd bet on it."

"He wouldn't lie about it, would he?"

"Sure he would. Why not?"

"I don't know. I just don't think he would. Not to us."

"Well, maybe you're right. But married or not, I'll bet you money he doesn't go back to Palm Beach."

"You think he'll end up in Honolulu like he said?"

"Not unless Honolulu comes to get him. Chet's been on his way to Hawaii since he was ten years old. Or New Zealand or Chile or someplace. But it's all talk. He wears himself out making plans. Then he's too tired to go."

"Don't you think he was in California and everyplace like he says?"

"Sure, I do. But I don't think he liked it. He likes Kittredge. That's why he came back. Wouldn't surprise me if he never left there again. Chet's a funny guy. He talks big but he's scared of all kinds of things."

"Maybe he wouldn't come to Nebraska then."

"Oh, that's different. If we're there, he'll come. He'd better or we'll have him crated up and shipped."

The afternoon traffic was light on 219. Kermit stood on the highway shoulder with his thumb up and Jossie sat back from the road at a picnic table writing on a small pad of paper. After a while, Kermit called over to her. "What are you doing?"

"Writing to Agnes."

"That's not such a great idea."

"Yes, it is," she said. "You'll see."

They waited by the highway till after four thirty. Finally, an interstate semi hauling structural steel picked them up. When they climbed into the cab, the driver said, "How far you going?"

"Bluefield."

"Well, I have to cut over west to Beckley. I can take you seventeen miles south to Ronceverte or I can drop you over at Hinton and you can take Highway Twenty down from there."

"We'll go on to Hinton, I guess."

Just before they got off at the junction east of Hinton, Jossie said to the driver, "How far do you have to go today?"

"I'll stop an hour in Beckley, then dog it straight on through to Knoxville."

She took the stamped envelope out of her pocket. "Would you be able to mail this when you get to Knoxville?"

"Be glad to. I'll mail it in Beckley if you'd rather."

"No, Knoxville's better, I think."

While they stood by the highway watching the truck roll away, Kermit said, "You're smart as a whip, aren't you?"

"Maybe," she said. "We'll see."

43

That night they camped at the north edge of Bluestone State Park. They'd bought baloney and potato chips and bread at a grocery store on the road. They had a cold supper so they wouldn't have to show a fire.

"The sign said 'No camping except on posted camp grounds.' Is this a posted camp ground?" Jossie said.

"No."

"Then why did we stop here?"

"Because it's not a posted camp ground."

"If I want a smart-ass answer, I know where to go," she said.

After they finished eating, Kermit collected the trash, put it in a sack, and buried it forty yards away from where they were camping. When he got back, Jossie had spread their blankets on the grass. "I've been thinking about Chet," she said. "What you said before."

"What about it?"

"I don't know. I used to think when you knew somebody for a long time that meant you knew everything about them. But it doesn't work that way, does it?"

"Not very often."

"Chet's so straight-out and open, always cracking jokes and making faces, it's easy to forget he's got a serious side."

"Chet's practically *all* serious. That's why he kids around so much."

"Is that why he drinks too?"

"No. I think he does that because it tastes good to him."

"What happened to that girl he was going to marry? The rich one from Wheeling."

"They broke up, I guess."

"Did he tell you why?"

"Some problem with her folks, the way I remember it. They had other plans for her."

While they talked, Jossie took off her clothes, folded each piece carefully, and made a neat pile with the rest of their gear. Then she pulled one of Kermit's T-shirts over her head like a nightgown and slipped under the blanket. Kermit draped his clothes across a stump and got under the blanket in his shorts.

"Didn't she have any say about it?" Jossie said.

"You still talking about Chet's girl?"

"Yes."

"She didn't want to go against her folks, I guess."

"Are all rich people like that?"

"I don't know. I don't know any rich people."

"Well, anyway, it's a shame."

There was a long silence then, soft forest sounds all around them, and occasional far-off car horns on the highway.

Finally, Kermit said, "I guess you're just going to lie there talking all night. Is that it?"

"I'm not saying a word."

"I guess you're just going to lie there and not say anything all night."

"Does that mean you want me to pay some attention to you?"

"I was thinking about it."

She raised herself on one elbow and looked down at him.

"Anything special you had in mind?"

"Why don't you try some different things?" he said. "And I'll pick out one I like."

She moved closer under the blanket and put her arms around him.

"That's a start," he said.

44

The morning was cool and damp and soft gray, autumn folding in early, the sun not yet up in the east, tree trunks black and shining in the dimness, hedges and thickets silver with cold drops that weren't quite frost, and ground fog rolling across the floor of the forest.

Jossie shivered under the blankets, squirmed closer to Kermit, put her arm around him and slipped back into sleep. Almost. Some soundless signal opened her eyes. Standing just over her, two feet back from the edge of the blanket, was a man, holding a rifle. Stocky, wearing a red hunting shirt, he said, "Well I'll be damned. Look what we found here, Barney."

As she looked up, frozen silent, still half-asleep, a second man, taller, also carrying a rifle, stepped up beside the first one. "I think we found a matched set of something-or-other."

"Which are they, Glen, hippies or hillbillies?"

Jossie put her hand on Kermit's shoulder and shook him.

"Wake up, Kermit. Come on, honey. Wake up."

Glen grinned down at them and said, "That's right, honey. Time to get up."

Kermit turned on his back and opened his eyes. He sat up abruptly, supporting himself on one elbow.

"Easy," Barney said. "Take it easy now, honey."

"That's not his name," Glen said. "His name's Kermit."

"Kermit? What kind of a name is that?"

"What do you guys want?" Kermit said.

"Nothing. We don't want anything."

"We were just walking through the woods here," Barney said, "getting ready to do some shooting."

"And we almost stepped on you and your girl friend."

"She's my wife," Kermit said.

"That's funny. I don't see a ring on her hand."

"She must be his wife, Barney. Otherwise they wouldn't be sacked in together. These are God-fearing people down here. This is what they call the Bible belt."

"I asked you before," Kermit said. "What do you want?"

"And I *told* you before. We don't want anything."

"We're just down here from Scranton. Doing some hunting."

"Well, you picked the wrong place," Kermit said. "This is a state park."

The two men looked at each other. "You hear that, Glen? Sounds like Kermit's a game warden. You a game warden, Kermit?"

"No, I'm not. I was just trying to do you a favor."

"That's nice of you. We appreciate it."

"Look," Kermit said. "Why don't you go ahead with your business and leave us alone?"

"He's not very friendly, is he?" Barney said.

"Doesn't seem to be. His wife acts friendlier than he does."

"Just go away and stop bothering us," Jossie said.

"Now she's not friendly either."

"Nothing to worry about, miss . . ."

"Missus," Glen said.

"That's right, missus. We're just a couple of ordinary guys. Away from home for a few days, breathing the fresh air and having a little fun."

"Just get the hell away from here," Kermit said, "and let us be."

"Now, wait a minute, Sunshine. Don't start getting nasty." Barney eased back a step or two. "I think you'd better crawl out of those blankets and let us take a look at you. If you're about to turn mean, I want to see what we're up against."

Glen made a gesture with his rifle. "Come on, kid. Pile out of there."

"Go ahead, Kermit," Jossie said. "Don't start anything."

"That's good advice, Kermit. You listen to what she says."

Kermit pushed the blanket back and stood up.

"That's better," Glen said. "Now back off four or five steps."

Kermit stepped back, the grass damp and cold under his bare feet.

"That's it. Stop right there."

The two men studied him carefully. "He doesn't look too mean, does he?"

"Not to me," Barney said. "Combs his hair with water and sleeps in his underwear."

"How about your friend here, your wife or whatever you want to call her . . . does she sleep in her underwear, too?"

"I'm warning you, mister," Kermit said.

"There he goes again."

"We wouldn't hurt her," Barney said. "We wouldn't hurt anybody. We're executive people. Aluminum business. Married men with kids. Right, Glen?"

"That's right. We're taxpayers. Family men. The kind of people who drive station wagons."

"It's just that we've never been in this part of the country before and we're inquisitive about it. You see a man in the woods sleeping in his underwear it's only natural to want to know what his wife sleeps in."

"My guess is she's wearing pajamas," Glen said.

"No, I don't think so. I'd bet on a flannel nightgown." He turned toward Jossie. "It's up to you now, missus. You're the only one who can satisfy our curiosity."

"You guys are gonna be sorry for this," Kermit said.

Glen made a half-turn toward him. "You just stand quiet over there and don't worry."

"Come on, ma'am," Barney said. "We're waiting."

When Jossie looked toward Kermit, Glen said, "It's all right. Your boy friend's right here to look after you."

Jossie deliberately folded the top blanket back and stood up. Kermit's shirt hung loose on her to her mid-thighs.

"Well, I'll be damned," Barney said. "She sleeps in her underwear too."

"No, she doesn't. She sleeps in *his* underwear."

Kermit turned his head slightly, glanced toward the pile of gear fifteen feet away, his shotgun, wrapped in burlap, tilted against a tree trunk. Jossie stood side-view to him, shivering in the gray light, holding the cotton shirt down against her legs. Keeping his eyes on her and the two men, Kermit shifted his feet, easing toward the shotgun, a few inches at a time.

Staring at Jossie, Glen said, "You've got a cute little wife here. You ought to buy her some warm pajamas. But I have to admit she looks pretty cute without them. Don't you think she's cute, Barney?"

"Cute as a bug. But there's one thing bothering me. That looks like a government issue T-shirt she's wearing."

"It sure does."

"Well, then, unless this little girl's in the army. . . . Are you a member of the armed forces, honey?"

Jossie looked at him and didn't answer.

"It's *my* shirt, for Christ's sake," Kermit said.

Barney ignored him. "It looks to me as if this young lady's got hold of some army property."

"Looks that way to me," Glen said.

"In a case like this, concerned citizens and all, don't you think we have a duty to return that property to its rightful owners?"

"No question about it in my mind."

Barney turned back to Jossie, took a half-step toward her, and held out his hand. "Sorry, miss. You'll have to hand it over."

"The hell she does," Kermit said.

Glen swung his rifle around. For the first time he pointed it straight at Kermit's chest. "Don't get nervous, kid. Like we said, we don't want to hurt you. But the situation is different now. We have a patriotic duty here. I mean if somebody *did* get hurt it wouldn't be our fault, would it?"

"It's all right, Kermit," Jossie said. "If they want the shirt that bad, they can have it." She stood there, looking at the two men. Then she pulled the shirt up and slipped it over her head. She stood there in the morning light, slender and pale and beautiful, the mist still hanging like a curtain from the trees, ground fog rolling slowly across the grass.

The men stood frozen, staring at her, as she slowly folded the shirt into a thick, neat square. "You want it," she said, "you've got it."

As she tossed the shirt toward them, as it unfolded and fluttered loosely through the air, Kermit made his move. In two swift steps he was behind the tree and out again, holding the shotgun in front of him. "All right, you bastards, let's start over."

"What the hell is that thing?" Barney said.

"It's a shotgun, you son-of-a-bitch."

"Doesn't look to me like . . ."

Kermit angled the barrel slightly and triggered a

charge into the ground. Dirt and leaves and gravel sprayed up against the two men as buckshot ripped into the earth at their feet. They dropped their rifles and stumbled back, their legs gone suddenly soft at the knees, their hands held up, open-palmed, around their shoulders.

Jossie picked up a blanket and wrapped it around her.

"Are you all right?" Kermit said.

She nodded her head and said, "Watch yourself, honey."

"It's all right. Without those rifles in their hands, they don't have much to say. You have anything to say, boys?"

"Don't get the wrong idea," Barney said, his eyes fixed on the shotgun. "We weren't going to hurt anybody."

"Just having a little fun," Glen said.

"You hear that, Jossie?" Kermit said. "Did you have any fun?"

"No."

"Neither did I."

"Look, we're sorry," Barney said. "Maybe it wasn't such a good idea. But we didn't mean . . ."

"It was kind of a game," Glen said.

"Sure it was," Kermit said. "I could see that. Sort of a strip-tease game. Is that what you'd call it?"

The men didn't answer. "Well, that's what *I'd* call it. And since you guys seemed to get a kick out of it, I think we ought to keep it going. What do you think, Jossie?"

"Sure. Why not?"

Kermit stepped closer to the two men, brought the gun up level, and said, "Start stripping."

"Oh, now, wait a minute," Glen said.

Kermit moved in another half-step. "I mean right down to the skin. And I mean right now."

White-faced and shivering, their eyes riveted to Kermit, the two men started to take off their clothes.

45

On an interstate bus, orange trimmed with red, speeding south on Highway 20 toward Bluefield, Kermit and Jossie sat in seats near the front, their blanket rolls stashed overhead, Jossie laughing and dabbing at her eyes with Kermit's handkerchief. "God, that was funny. That was the funniest thing I ever saw."

"They didn't think so."

"I guess not. They were so scared I thought they'd pee down their legs."

"Good enough for them."

"I'll never forget the way they looked. Standing there shaking with their white bellies sticking out, trying to cover themselves with their hands."

"They got off easy, the bastards."

"You think they'll find their car?" ·

"If they look, they will. It's only a mile down the road from where they'd parked it."

"That's a long way when you're naked."

"Good. It'll give them a little time to think."

"I thought I'd split when you made them run off through the woods like that. They looked like a Tom-and-Jerry cartoon, running from one tree to the next, trying to keep us from seeing them."

"They're a couple of specimens, all right."

"At least they learned a lesson, I'll bet."

"I doubt it," Kermit said. "Soon as they get in their car, with their clothes on and those rifles back in their hands, they'll be the same horses' asses they were this morning."

Outside the bus window the country was desolate, ravaged by neglect and ill-use, sprinkled with abandoned houses and falling barns and studded with the skeletons of junked cars, a rusted chassis under every tree.

Looking out, Jossie saw very few people. An occasional man, lean and wasted, stood motionless by the road. Or an empty-faced woman holding a child, knee-deep in a yard of tangled grass and weeds. Poorly dressed, underfed and expressionless, the people seemed stunned by yesterday and resigned to tomorrow.

"What happened down here?" Jossie said.

"Same thing that's happened lots of places. People just laid down and gave up. If you think this is bad, wait till you see Bluefield."

"But there's work in Bluefield."

"Some days there's work. Some days there's not. Some people get it and most people don't. It's like every place else."

46

Jim August parked his car across the street from Jernegan's store. Leaving the police radio turned up, static crackling behind him, he got out, slammed the car door behind him, and walked toward the store.

"Fucking the dog, Dude. I caught you at it."

Dude Jernegan, in his fifties, thinning hair, pale, an indoor man, deep furrows in his flat cheeks, broken veins in his nose, sat on a bench on the porch, leaning back against the pine siding by the screen door.

"You're a great one to talk," he said. "Never worked a day in your life. Sliding around in that car all day, looking at yourself in the rear-view glass, and scouting for pussy."

Jim sat down on the edge of the porch and lit a cigarette. "Where's all the regulars? It's not often I catch you without some company."

"The grocery customers came in early and I sold out

on beer an hour or so ago. I guess everybody went home to take a nap and wait for a fresh batch to ice up."

"You ought to get yourself a bigger icebox."

"I ought to get myself a lot of things but I'm not likely to."

"To tell you the truth," Jim said, "I'm just as glad I found you by yourself. I wanted to ask you a favor."

"What's that?"

"Police business. It's about the mail."

"What about it?"

"Well, since you're the postal agent here, you sort through all the letters that come into Kittredge. Isn't that right?"

Jernegan nodded. "Either I do or my wife does. We split it up. If I get snowed under with my other work, Nonnie helps out with the mailbag."

"Here's the problem. We're trying to locate Kermit Docker. I guess everybody around here knows that. So if there's any chance he might be in touch with his sister, or if Jossie's writing to her mom, we need to know about it. It would help us a lot to see those postmarks so we'd know where they're sent from. Lieutenant Hadley up at the police barracks in Buckhannon told me to check it out with you and I said I would. I told him you and I were pretty good friends and I thought you'd be anxious to help us out."

"All you want to know is who's getting what mail and where it comes from. Is that it?"

Jim nodded. "Just Kermit's sister and Jossie's mother. Those two places."

"Sounds simple enough . . ."

"That's what I thought you'd say."

". . . but I can't do it, Jim. Can't do it and won't do it."

Jim took a drag on his cigarette, held it in, then let it trail out slowly. "Why's that, Dude?"

"It's none of my business what comes in the mail for

people. And it's none of your business either."

"It's not a personal thing. Like I said, this is police work we're talking about."

"I don't care if it is. I'm not tinkering with private mail for you or anybody else."

Jim stood up and ground his cigarette out on the porch floor. "I appreciate what you're saying, Dude, but this is a special case."

"Special for you maybe but not for me."

"I mean I've got a job to do."

"So have I. And I don't need you or anybody else telling me how to do it. You've been in this county three or four years. I've been here all my life. I never had any police trouble and I don't aim to have any. But that don't mean I have to kiss some lieutenant's ass up at the police barracks." He stood up and opened the screen door. "That's how I feel about it now and that's how I'll feel about it a year from now." He went inside then and the screen door slapped shut behind him.

Jim crossed the porch and sat down on the bench. He smoked another cigarette and stared out at the street. Finally he stood up, crossed over to his car, started the engine, and drove off.

47

The bus came into Bluefield at the northeast corner of town and turned west down Princeton Avenue, paralleling the Norfolk and Western tracks, the air heavy and gray with smoke and coal dust, a continuing din of railroad cars screeching and pounding together in the midday heat.

"Jesus," Jossie said. "I can't believe it."

"This is Bluefield."

"It's nothing but dirt and railroad tracks."

The bus pulled into a grimy bus station at the intersection of Princeton and Poplar, where Highway 52 buttonhooks in from the northwest. Kermit carried their gear into the terminal, and Jossie stayed with it while he got into line at the information window. When his turn came, a worn-out, red-eyed woman stared at him over the counter.

"Excuse me," Kermit said. "I'm looking for somebody who lives on Quigley Street. Where is that located?"

"Can't help you. Nothing but bus information here."

"It doesn't say that on the sign."

"Never mind what it says on the sign. This is a bus station. We just hand out *bus* information."

"Give me a break, lady. I'm tired and my wife is tired. We just came in on the bus and we don't know a damned soul here."

The woman dug a mint out of a foil-wrapped roll and put it in her mouth. "It's people like you that make it a long day." She put the mints back in her sweater pocket. "Whereabouts on Quigley?"

Kermit smoothed out a crumpled piece of paper on the counter top. "Twelve-oh-two it says here."

"You walk back down Princeton to Bland Road, turn right four or five traffic lights and you'll hit Quigley. Then left a couple blocks. You'll see it."

"How far is it?"

"A mile and a half maybe."

In a run-down, gritty neighborhood, it was a run-down house, a two-story frame building, tar-paper shingles nailed on over the siding, the yard as bare of grass as a paved street, surly cats in multiples, squares of cardboard replacing broken windowpanes, candy wrappers blowing, beer cans in corners, and two broken chairs leaning together on the front porch. By the door, a handwritten sign, ROOM AND BOARD, was nailed up.

"One thing sure. Your dad's not living fancy," Jossie said.

"No, I guess not."

They stepped up on the porch and Kermit knocked on the screen door. When Jossie leaned back against the porch railing, he said, "Are you tired?"

"I'm dragging for some reason. It must be this town. I'd be sipping Sterno through a straw if I lived here."

"What do you want?"

Kermit turned around and saw a heavy-set woman behind the screen door, barefoot, wearing a man's bathrobe, carrying a small, ugly dog.

"Hello," he said. The woman didn't answer and the dog began to growl. "I'm looking for a man named Archie Docker."

After a long pause the woman said, "Who's looking for him?"

"He wrote and said we could find him here."

"I said who's looking for him?"

"I'm his boy."

Her face came closer to the screen and she stared at Kermit and Jossie, taking in the details of their faces and clothing. Finally she said, "Maybe you are and maybe you ain't."

"If he's here, why don't you . . ."

"What's your name?"

"Docker. Kermit Docker. My middle name's Hollenbeck."

The dog kept growling while the woman stared at Kermit. "You stay here," she said. "I'll see if he's upstairs." She turned away and disappeared, leaving a scent of damp rot and boiled cabbage behind her.

"How'd you like to find her in your hope chest?" Kermit said.

"I wouldn't. What's the matter with her anyway?"

"She's lived too long, I guess."

"At least she could have asked us to come in."

"I just got a whiff of the inside. I think we're better off out here." He sat down on the railing, put his arm around Jossie, and kissed her on the forehead.

"So you're pooped out, huh?"

"Not all the way. Just frazzled around the edges."

"I guess maybe I've been paying too much attention to you."

"It's not that kind of tired," she said.

"Have to find you a convent where you can put on one of those nuns' outfits and rest up for a year or so."

"Screw you, big mouth."

"The trouble is you're too old for me. Just a little bit past your prime."

"I'll show you who's past somebody's prime." She reached out suddenly to grab him, he twisted away, laughing, and the woman's voice hissed out through the screen. "Stop that! Stop that orneriness on my porch!"

Kermit moved back up to the door. "Sorry, ma'am. We were just kidding around a little."

"I keep a good place here for decent people. I won't have trash like you tomcatting each other on my premises."

"What about my dad?" Kermit cut in.

"Lucky you're not in jail, you two."

"Just tell me if my dad's here."

From somewhere inside the house they heard a man's voice, low and rumbling. The woman changed directions abruptly and said, "There's a kind of a park down a ways to your right. He said he'd meet you there."

"Well, if it's all the same to you, we'll sit and wait for him here."

"No, you won't. It's *not* all the same to me. I don't allow any loafing around in front of my place. You just pick up your junk there and make tracks."

Kermit signaled Jossie with a look and she stood up.

"You're a nice friendly woman," Jossie said. "You remind me of my mother."

She and Kermit walked down the steps to the sidewalk. When Jossie turned back, the woman still stood in the doorway, like a hangman.

"And if you think that's a compliment, you're crazy," Jossie said.

The door slammed behind them and the dog yelped as they walked off down the sidewalk.

48

In the designated park, stripped and vandalized, broken benches, trampled shrubs, and trees with dead limbs, a layer of cinders and grit over everything, Kermit and Jossie sat on a backless slat bench, between them Archie Docker, defeated and brutalized, iron-gray hair, whisker stubble, and sunken cheeks.

"The police been to see me twice," he was saying. "That's why I wanted to steer you away from Garnet's place."

"Garnet?" Jossie said.

"Garnet Basenfelder. That's the woman you were talking to a while ago."

"You mean the military police came to see you?" Kermit said.

"No. I didn't say military. They was regular police. From Bluefield here. They chewed me over good. Trying to find out if I knew where to locate you."

"What did you tell them?"

"I said as far as I knew, you was still soldiering someplace over in Germany."

"What did they say to that?"

"They said I was to get in touch with them the first word I had from you."

"Beats me," Kermit said.

"How's that?"

"They're sure going to a lot of bother just to get me back in the army."

"That's not what they're after," Archie said. "They claim you killed a man."

"They *what?*" Jennie said.

"First thing they told me was that Kermit had killed somebody up in Kittredge."

"You sure you got it straight?" Kermit said.

"Exact. I'm telling you just what they told me," Archie said. "They said you killed Chet."

"Chet Mobley?"

"That's what they said."

"They're crazy. Chet's not dead. He got cracked on the head by an M.P. but he's a long way from being dead."

"He's dead, Kermit. They buried him two weeks ago." He took a folded envelope out of his shirt pocket. "It's all right here in your sister's letter."

Jossie took the envelope, pulled the letter out, and scanned it quickly. "My God," she said.

She looked at Kermit and he said, "What's it say?"

"Chet died the day after Kermit took him to the hospital. Never came to himself to talk or anything from the time they brought him in. Hemorrhage of the brain, the doctor said . . ."

"Jesus . . . I can't believe it."

"The doctor told you it wasn't serious at all," Jossie said. "Wasn't that what he said?"

Kermit nodded his head. "He told me Chet would be on his feet the next day."

"But why would they think . . . I mean you didn't have

anything to do with his being hurt."

"Because I brought him in, I guess."

"No, I don't think that's it," Archie said. "Agnes wrote about that too. Read on a little piece."

Jossie looked at the letter again, turned a page over. "Here it is," she said. "Those two army people went to the state police and told them they'd seen the whole thing happen. They said Kermit and Chet were jawing back and forth and starting to fist-fight when they pulled up in front of the house. They said Kermit picked up a stick of wood and hit Chet over the head with it."

The three of them sat silent, looking down at the ground. Finally Jossie said, "I can't get it straight in my head. Why would they lie like that?"

"To save their own ass," Kermit said. "That's why." He stood up and said, "Let's go."

A few blocks from the park, Archie steered them down a narrow street, small frame cottages on either side, weathered and neglected. "I got a friend has a little house up the way here. She can take you in for a few days and not let on to anybody about it."

49

"It's nothing to get mad at me about," Jossie said.

"I'm not mad at you," Kermit said. "I told you that."

They were sitting in a second-story room, a narrow bed and one straight chair, a torn paper shade and no curtains, stained wallpaper, and worn-through linoleum on the floor.

They'd been there for eight days, never going outside, eating peanut butter sandwiches and drinking milk out of cartons, talking for hours, then sitting silent, measuring their options, making plans, rejecting them, counting their money three times a day, trying to find a destination and some way of reaching it.

"I'm not bossing you," she said. "I wasn't trying to tell you what to do."

"I didn't say you were."

"I just meant we can't sit here forever."

"I know that."

"I think we have to go back and tell them the truth."

"I know that's what you think," he said. "You already told me that."

"I don't know what else we *can* do."

"All right, suppose we did go back. What makes you think they'd believe us?"

"They *have* to believe us. It's the *truth.*"

"What about the M.P.'s' story?"

"They're lying."

"Course they are. *You* know that and *I* know it. But nobody else does. It's our word against theirs. How can we make anybody believe that those guys got in a fight with Chet? They weren't even looking for him. They were looking for *me. He* wasn't AWOL. *I* was. And if I *didn't* do anything wrong, why did I run away? *They* didn't run. *I* did. That's the way people look at things."

"But won't they listen to me?"

"Why would they? You ran away, too."

She got up and walked to the window, looked out around the shade at the chaos of the backyard. "I don't know what to think," she said. "I feel like somebody nailed me in a box."

He walked over and stood behind her with his arms around her waist. "We'll work it out. Just try to stop worrying."

"I would if I could. But I *can't* stop. I'm worried sick. If we keep running, they're bound to catch you sooner or later. Then it'll be worse even than it is now."

"No, it won't. That's where you're wrong. Cause they're not going to catch me."

"How do you know that?"

He turned her around to face him. "Because I *do*. That's why. We'll get up to Charleston or Parkersburg or some good-sized place where nobody knows us. I'll find some kind of a job and we'll squirrel away some money for a few weeks. Then we'll head on out west the way we talked about."

"Can't they find you in a city as easy as they could here?"

"Not a chance. Everybody looks alike in the city."

She stood there looking at him, trying to believe. Finally she said, "Maybe we could go to Huntington. My brother's living there."

That night they talked it over with Archie and the next afternoon he came to see them again.

"I got you a ride up to Huntington. Leaving tomorrow morning at eight sharp."

"How'd you manage that?"

"A guy I met at the union hall. Runs his own truck back and forth between here and there."

"What did you tell him?"

"Not much. Just said you were my kid and you're broke and you and your wife need a ride up north."

"What did he say?"

"He's tickled to have you along. He's a bullshit artist. Likes to have somebody to tell his stories to."

50

In Melvin Culp's garage, late afternoon, Agnes reached down and hefted the baby out of her playpen. Melvin leaned back against his workbench, looking uncomfortable, and Jim August, arms folded, stood beside him.

"I thought it was nobody's business what comes to a

person in the mail," Agnes said.

"Regular practice, that's true," Jim said. "But this is what you call a special case."

"Special or not," Melvin said. "You can't expect Agnes to talk against her own brother."

"It's not what *I* expect that counts. It's the law. If you hold back what you know, that's looked on as aiding a criminal. Aiding and abetting."

"Kermit's no criminal and you know it," Agnes said.

"The law says he is. You know what he did."

"I don't believe that stuff," Agnes said. "And I never will."

"Why'd he run away then?"

Agnes shifted the baby from one arm to the other. "I don't know. But he must have had a reason."

Jim turned to Melvin. "You'd better have a talk with her and tell her to help us out. I wouldn't like to see you people get in any trouble."

"I'm not telling her what to do," Melvin said. "If she doesn't want to talk against Kermit, I can't blame her. If it was my brother, I'd feel the same way about it."

"But there's no use lying about it. We *know* she got the letter."

"No, you don't either," Agnes said. "Dude told us what he said to you . . . that a person's mail is private business and he wouldn't tell you what *anybody* got in the mail."

"That's right," Jim said. "That's what he told me. But the district post office up in Buckhannon feels different about it. We had a man checking every piece of mail that came through to Kittredge and he said there was a letter for you. No question about it."

He turned to Melvin. "You see what I mean? I'm not just blowing bubbles. I've got facts. So why won't she admit it?"

There was a long silence, Agnes very busy adjusting

the baby's clothes and smoothing her hair. Finally, she looked up and said, "All right. What if I did get a letter? I still don't think it's any concern of yours. But if you'll stop pestering us, I'll admit it. I got a letter."

"I'd like to see it," Jim said.

"You can't. I tore it up and threw it away."

"Was it from Kermit?"

"No. Jossie wrote it. It was mailed from Knoxville over a week ago."

"What did she say?"

"Not much of anything. Just that they were going straight on through to Mexico. I expect they're down there by now."

51

Inside the cab of the trailer-truck, Tim Cable, a beefy man in his late forties, high color and electric energy, was driving north, mid-morning, toward Huntington, State Highway 10, laughing and talking, Kermit and Jossie on the seat beside him.

"It's good to have somebody riding along. Keeps me from talking to myself. I hired a man I didn't need for two years. Just to keep me company. He was a nice kid, too. Name of Ratliff. Herman Ratliff. But I had to let him go. Couldn't handle those wages every week."

"How often you make this run?" Kermit said.

"I never *stop* making it. Back and forth all the time. Soon as I get a truckload, away I go. Same thing coming back. Load up and take off."

"Sounds like they keep you jumping."

"Oh, I'm busy, all right. Too busy. Mostly because I work cheap. I could always jack up my rates but if I did I might lose trade. Then I'd get so jumpy I'd be worse off."

"Well, at least you're your own boss."

"No doubt about it. And it's a good thing I am. Otherwise I'd have been canned long ago."

Jossie was sitting with her head back and her eyes closed, air blowing through the half-open window on her face. Cable glanced over at her and said, "Is your wife feeling all right?"

"Oh, sure. She's fine."

"She doesn't look too frisky."

"Well, she gets woozy sometimes if she rides in a car too long at a stretch. But when she's got some air in her face, she manages all right." He leaned close to Jossie and said, "How you doing?"

"Plugging along," she said, keeping her eyes closed.

"There's like a bed up here behind the seat if you want to stretch out."

"I think I'll stick it out here."

At eleven o'clock they pulled into a truck stop outside Chapmanville.

"How about some food?" Cable said. "It's on me."

"Nothing for me," Jossie said. "You two go ahead. I'll wait out here in the truck."

Inside, at the counter, Cable and Kermit drank coffee and ate a platter of sausage and eggs, and soda biscuits with gravy. And Cable kept talking.

"My third wife was a redhead. And so was the fourth one. At least she dyed her hair red. I never found out what color it really was. She didn't stick around that long. By the time her roots grew out she was long gone."

"*Four* wives. Boy, that sounds like a lot of wives," Kermit said.

"Four is nothing. The truth is I've had five. Just split up with the last one during the winter. And I've got number six picked out already. I'm like Will Rogers, I guess. Never met a woman I didn't like."

When they came back out to the truck, Jossie had

crawled up behind the seat, covered herself with a blanket, and gone to sleep. When Cable talked now, heading north on the highway again, he kept his voice down.

"I'll bet you don't remember Will Rogers, do you?"

"I've heard my folks talk about him."

"Me too. I don't remember him that much first-hand. But I've done some reading about him and listened to some records he made. He was a funny man, all right. Nice man, too, they say. Loved horses. Used to play a lot of polo. I read somewhere that he had his own polo field. I guess . . . oh-oh, here comes trouble." He nudged Kermit and said, "See that bullhorn down there under the dash? Hand it to me, quick."

Driving with one hand, he angled the bullhorn through the open window toward a truck coming up in the southbound lane. "Hello, you thieving bastard."

From the other truck as it raced past, an answering bullhorn voice. "Fuck you, you father-grabber."

Cable passed the bullhorn back to Kermit, laughing and coughing and thumping the steering wheel. "That son-of-a-bitch. You can't top him. Fire a BB gun at him and he blasts you with a cannon. Known him since I was a kid. We started hauling together and we're both still at it. Only difference is, I'm honest and he's crooked as a dog's hind leg. He handles a lot more money than I do but by the time he's through paying people off, I have to give him money for his fuel bill. You talk about wild-assed, he invented it. Drink all night and play stud poker all day, women hanging on him like a bunch of snakes."

"Does he get married a lot, too?"

"Married? Not him. He thinks anybody that spends more than two nights with the same woman is losing his nerve."

"How do the women like that?"

"They're hogs for it. Can't get enough abuse. They all think they're gonna *change* him. But it works the other way around. He treats them so lousy they never get over him. Just the opposite from me. I treat women so nice they get bored. But . . . that's the way I am. Too late to change now."

Part Four

52

"I thought maybe Mom wrote you that Kermit was home," Jossie said. She was sitting in her brother Jack's house with Jack, a short, thin thirty-year-old man; Rose, his wife; and Kermit.

Jack shook his head. "Not her. I haven't had a word from her in over a year."

"Be two years Christmas," Rose said. She was a delicate girl with honey hair, pale skin, tiny wrists and ankles, twenty-two years old, and thirty pounds overweight.

"It's almost that long," Jack said, "since I heard anything from Dad."

"He sent a card for your birthday," Rose said. "A year ago last month."

Kermit listened carefully. He knew what Jossie was doing. Trying to find out how much they'd heard, fishing to see if they knew about Chet's death. "I guess you don't hear from anybody around Kittredge, then," she said.

"Not a soul. Been away now for three or four years and it's like I never lived there."

"Four years last March," Rose said.

Jack went to the kitchen and came back with two bottles of beer. He opened them and set one down in front of Kermit. "So you went over the hill, huh?"

"That's right."

"Wish I'd had the guts to do it. Wasted four good years of my life. And half the time I was in the stockade. I never could get used to that army shit, taking orders from whatever shavetail, snot-nose bastard happened along. I used to get busted breakfast, dinner, and supper. Every time I turned around. What I should have done is take off, the way you're doing. That's the only way to beat it."

"If you don't get caught," Kermit said.

"Don't worry about that. We'll outmaneuver the bastards. You'll be all right here for a while. We'll tell people you're my brother. That way nobody gets nosy about what your name is."

"What about work?" Jossie said.

"I don't know," Jack said. "That could be tough. Social Security cards and all that crap."

"Couldn't you ask at the warehouse?" Rose said.

"We need to get a little money together," Kermit said.

"Well, I'll see what I can find out. Maybe I could get you a chance to unload some trucks. They don't keep records on those jobs. Part-time, they call it. No medical or tax deductions or anything."

"I'd be much obliged for whatever you can do," Kermit said.

Next day, at the Dixon Foods Warehouse, between the C. and O. tracks and the river, Kermit walked out through a loading door and on down the long platform where half a dozen trucks were being loaded or unloaded. Just before he reached the steps going down to ground level, Jack came out through another doorway and caught up with him.

"How'd it go?"

"Good," Kermit said. "He's a nice guy. Said I could start work in the morning."

"I told you he was a buddy of mine. Did he say how long it would be for?"

"He wants to see how I pan out. Then we'll talk about how long."

That night after supper, Jossie and Kermit walked around the neighborhood near Jack's house, people on their porches, children running on the sidewalk, bluegrass music drifting out through doors and windows, the smells of cooking and fresh-cut lawns and spilled gasoline in the air.

"I can't get over how lucky we are," Jossie said.

"We're not lucky. *I'm* lucky."

"I know it. That's what Agnes said about you."

"I am a lucky duck."

"It's really going to work out, isn't it?"

"I told you it would. Didn't I tell you that?"

"How long you think we'll stay here?"

"Six weeks. Two months maybe. Long enough to collect some traveling money."

"Let's go as soon as we can."

"We will."

Three days later, late in the afternoon, Kermit and Jack came out of the warehouse together, walked across the parking lot, out the gate, and down the street to the city bus stop.

"I was talking to Jaycoxe today," Jack said. "He tells me you're a steady worker."

"You just have to keep plugging. God knows it doesn't take any brains to speak of."

"You keep it up, he says you might get a shot at some overtime."

"Yeah, that's what he told me."

The bus rolled up and stopped. They got on and found seats in the back. "Overtime," Jack said. "That's the ticket. Time-and-a-half you get. I lost out on that when they made me a checker. But you . . . next thing you know, you'll be rich and stuck-up. Not talking to anybody."

53

Wes Obuchowsky and Francis Wick, veteran plainclothes men on the Bluefield police force, stood on the boarding house steps on a gray, sultry day—August weather in late September—talking to Archie Docker.

"We're not calling you a liar," Wick said, "but it's hard to swallow that a man don't know any more about his own kid than you do."

"We told you before," Obuchowsky said, "the first word you hear from him, we want to know about it."

"I remember you said that," Archie said.

"You sure you didn't forget to tell us something?"

"I've got no reason to lie to anybody."

"Maybe not. But one of the boarders here told us that somebody came looking for you."

"When was that?" Archie said.

"I don't know. Some time back."

"Who told you anything like that?"

"Just somebody here in the house. He saw a young fella and a girl talking to you. He got the idea they might be relatives of yours."

Archie measured some tobacco into his pipe, tamped it carefully into the bowl with his finger.

"What about it?" Obuchowsky said.

"That was my brother's boy. He and his wife stopped by on their way to Akron. He's promised some work up there."

"What's your brother's name? We'd like to doublecheck this with him."

"Joseph."

"Where does he live?"

"Used to live up in the peninsula. Near Romney. But he's been dead for close to eight years now."

The policemen looked at each other. Then Wick said, "This nephew of yours, is he in Akron now?"

"Far as I know, he is. I haven't heard."

"And you wouldn't know how we could locate him up there?"

"No, I wouldn't."

"And you're dead sure," Obuchowsky said, "that you haven't had any word from your own boy."

"Just what I told you before, the letter my daughter had from him. Far as we know, he's in Mexico."

54

In their upstairs bedroom at Jack's house, Kermit sat on a straight chair watching Jossie iron their clean clothes. "I know what you mean," he said. "The same things keep going through *my* head. But you have to try and forget it."

"I *do* try. Seems like that's *all* I do. But I can't stop thinking about him."

"I can't either."

"I just can't get myself to believe he's dead."

"I can't either."

"Every time I hear a door open I expect him to come banging in, talking some new kind of craziness. I can't figure all that coming to a stop. I don't know what it would be like being in Kittredge with no chance of seeing Chet there."

She folded the shirt she'd been ironing and unplugged the iron from the wall. "I want to show you something," she said. She opened the top drawer of the bureau and took out a pocket-size spiral-bound notebook. She handed it to Kermit.

"It belonged to Chet," she said. "I just found it this morning. It was crammed clear down in the bottom of the motorcycle bag. First I thought it was yours. Then I saw his name on it."

"What is it, a diary or something?"

"No. It's not personal. Not like that." She took the book back from him. "Here, let me show you something." She leafed quickly through the pages. "It's like he used it for writing down what he thought about things. It seems like some of it goes back to when he was in school up at New River. Here," she said, "this is what I was looking for. It says 'Notes for a Speech.'" She handed the notebook to Kermit again. "Read it out loud," she said.

"Why can't you people wake up? There ought to be two million letters dumped on the White House steps every Monday morning." Kermit's voice was flat and low-pitched. "Maybe we won't get the answers we want, but at least somebody has to ask the questions. Who says a working man has to be taxed to death when a lot of rich people don't pay taxes at all? Show me that paragraph in the Bill of Rights. Why is it that Denmark and Sweden and Holland and Norway can take care of their old people and sick people and poor people and we can't? Why are people dying when they wouldn't have to? How come a soldier or a policeman or a man in prison gets free medical care and I don't? Why are little kids going hungry, for Christ's sake? Why is there so much money for killing and not enough for food? Why do we listen to lunatics?'"

Kermit closed the book and looked up at Jossie.

55

"You can fool yourself if you want to, but you're not fooling me any. You've been sick every morning since you got here." Rose was slicing carrots in her kitchen while Jossie washed the breakfast dishes.

"No, I haven't either."

"You just threw up, didn't you?"

"My stomach's a little funny. That's all."

"And you threw up yesterday morning, too." She waited for Jossie to answer but she didn't. "And I'll bet ten dollars your time's late."

"A little bit."

"How late?"

"I don't know."

"Yes, you do," Rose said.

"A week or so, maybe."

"A month or so is more like it."

"No, it's not," Jossie said.

"Tell me the truth. I know the signs, for God's sake."

Jossie came over and sat down at the table. "I missed last time and the time before," she said.

"That's what I thought."

56

Kermit sat on the tailgate of a truck, eating his lunch, Martin Haggard beside him. In his late fifties, Haggard was thin and bald and rawboned, pale gray eyes, several teeth missing, and skin weathered to the color of tobacco leaves.

"Cherry County," he said. "That's where I was mostly.

On a cattle ranch out there for more than two years. Nice people. A family named Swenson. Swedes. Been holding that land and running cattle on it since the Civil War. I liked it there. Liked it a lot. But . . . I got ants in my pants like I always do. So I took off. Went down to North Platte and worked in a grain elevator. A one-legged man owned it, fella named Senesac. Came from French people, he said. Well, I want to tell you, he kept me jumping. I earned every dime I made there. But the wages were good, and I got a day off every week except in harvest time. Then we really worked our asses off, round the clock, it seemed like. Anyway, after I left there, I was down in Thayer County for a while, then up to Grand Island, pretty much all over the state. I changed jobs a lot but I never went hungry. Always found work out there. And I met some decent people. Openhanded, a lot of them. Give you the fillings right out of their teeth. I'd go back out there in a minute. Had a lot of good times in Nebraska."

57

"The way you describe it, it sure sounds terrific," Jossie said. It was a Saturday afternoon, seven weeks since they'd arrived in Huntington, clear autumn days still, but a sharp chill in the air morning and evening.

"I'm just telling you the way it was described to me."

"Sounds like we might get out there and settle right down."

"I don't see why not," Kermit said, "if it's as good as Haggard says. According to him, Nebraska's the place."

They were downtown, killing time, looking in windows on one of the main business streets. They stopped for a moment in front of a pet store, half a dozen shepherd puppies tumbling over each other in the window. "You

think maybe we could have a dog when we get there?"
Jossie said.

"Sure. Why not? Have a couple if we want to. Dogs
and cats and kids and goldfish. And a baby alligator in
the bathtub."

"If we have a bathtub."

"That's right," Kermit said. "No bathtub, no alligator."

Jossie put her hand in her jacket pocket and walked
close to him. "I wasn't sure if you wanted to have kids.
We never talked about it."

"There's nothing to talk about, is there? It *happens*,
that's all. First thing you know, bingo."

"Well, you can plan for it if you want to. Put it off till
you're ready."

"I know that. But there's no use putting it off forever.
From what I hear, it's a good idea to do it when you're
young."

"Well, we're going to be young for quite a while yet,"
she said. "I mean it would probably be better if we settled in someplace first. Got our feet on the ground a little
bit."

"Yeah, I guess so."

They stopped in front of a furniture store, the plate-
glass window reflecting the street behind them. Jossie
squeezed Kermit's arm.

"Don't look around," she said. "I think there's a policeman watching us."

"Where?"

"Across the street. By that blue truck. You see him?"

"Yeah."

"Is he watching us?"

"I can't tell for sure."

They turned away from the window and walked slowly
down the street, keeping their backs to the policeman.

"Is he still watching?" Jossie said.

"I can't tell unless I turn square around and look at him."

"Don't do that. Let's go inside somewhere."

"What's that building we're coming to?"

"Looks like a public library."

They climbed the steps without looking back, and spun through the revolving doors. As soon as they were inside, a white-haired woman with a blue rinse on her short curls bustled up to them, eyes bright and magnified behind harlequin glasses.

"Are you here for the lecture?"

"Beg pardon?"

"I say the lecture's just started, if that's what you came for."

Jossie looked back outside through the glass door. Across the street she saw the policeman standing at the curb. "Yes," she said to the woman. "We'd certainly like to hear it."

As the woman steered them toward a heavy door at one side of the foyer, Kermit leaned close to Jossie and whispered, "We *would*?"

The woman eased the door open and put a forefinger to her lips. "Right in here. You only missed a little bit."

Except for some light spill from the projector, it was dark inside. A portable screen was set up at one end of the room and a tiny lady, also white-haired, stood at a lecture stand just beside it, facing an audience of fifteen or twenty elderly women perched on folding chairs. At the back of the room someone was operating the slide projector. Jossie and Kermit made giant silhouettes on the screen as they stumbled into the first empty chairs.

"Welcome, young folks," the woman at the lectern said. "Better late than never. We're usually a little short of young people here, but we're always glad to have them."

She changed back to her lecture voice then and took

up where she'd left off, half-turned toward the screen, a pointer in her left hand. "That's the mother, Mrs. James, in the center. Frank, her oldest boy, is on her left and Jesse's on the right, the one with the Buster Brown haircut. There was a sister, too, they say, but she's not in the picture. Maybe she was the one that *took* the picture. Anyway, they're pleasant-looking boys, aren't they? A person would never guess from looking at these faces what lay ahead. Slide, please."

The picture changed on the screen.

"Thank you, Helen. Now, you remember at my last lecture I mentioned the Younger boys. Here they are again, just to refresh your memory."

The picture changed again.

"And the Dalton brothers, of course. We heard about them last time, too. Slide."

Another picture change.

"And here's the Reno brothers. New faces, I expect, to most of you. The Renos were from Indiana and not so well known as some of the other outlaws. But history books say they staged the very first train robbery . . ."

Kermit leaned close to Jossie. "I don't *believe* this."

"Neither do I. Be quiet."

"Slide, please. Thank you," the lecturer said. "And here's Butch Cassidy and his bunch. As you can see, he doesn't look much like Paul Newman at all. Just in case you happened to see that movie. Howard and I went to see it, but I can't honestly say I liked it. It was entertaining, of course, and the music was catchy, but it didn't seem true to life to me. Too smart-alecky, I thought. Howard said they tried to make it too up-to-date was the trouble. Slide . . . and here's our main subject for today. Not a very good photograph. But it's the only one I could locate. They say he wasn't photographed a lot."

"I can see why," Jossie whispered.

"This young man was named William Bonney. But

everyone called him Billy. And history knows him as Billy the Kid. The books don't say whether he was called that in his lifetime. Or to his *face."* She paused to let that sink in. Then, "This picture makes it look as if he was left-handed. But some people say they just turned over the negative when the print was made. In other words, he may have been *right*-handed. But whichever hand he shot with, he managed to kill twenty-some men in his short life. By the way, Paul Newman also played *him* in a movie. I guess they like him for those outlaw parts because of his eyes. I've read that almost all the Western killers had blue eyes. Slide, please . . ."

A gray, scratched tintype of a weather-beaten lady flashed on.

"And here's Billy's mother. You can tell by looking at her that she never had an easy time of it. In those days, a woman was lucky if she lived to be forty. But she was a decent, God-fearing woman and Billy was very attached to her. From what we know about it he was a fine, loving son. It seems likely that if he hadn't loved his mother so much, he never would have turned out to be our most famous killer. On the other hand . . ."

It was getting dark in the streets when Kermit and Jossie came out of the library. As soon as they were down the steps to the sidewalk, they started to laugh. Imitating the white-haired lady, Kermit said, "It seems that Billy the Kid was very attached to his mother. Matter of fact, the first man he shot was his father . . ."

58

When they got home an hour later, their clothes and blankets were bundled together on the side porch. And Rose, by herself, was waiting for them in the kitchen. Her nose was red and her eyes were wet and she held a damp handkerchief balled up in her hand.

In front of her, on the kitchen table, was a small sheet of paper, Kermit's picture, in uniform, printed on it, and a line of black type under the picture: "Wanted for murder and desertion from the United States Army."

"I never saw Jack so mad," Rose kept saying. Jossie sat across the table from her looking stunned and Kermit leaned against the sink, stiff and silent. "I tried to get him to wait till you got home but he wouldn't do it. He said he didn't want to see you, either one of you. After he helped you as much as he could and fixed you up with a job and all, and then to find out you lied to us, to find out they had your picture up in the post office for killing somebody . . ." She started to cry. "Jack said we could have got in a lot of trouble for letting you stay here. We still could."

"But I *told* you, Rose, I *keep* telling you, it's not the *truth*. Kermit didn't kill anybody. I know. I was there."

"If I could tell Jack what happened," Kermit said.

"It's no use," Rose said. "He doesn't want to listen. You should have heard him. He was yelling at me like it was my fault. He grabbed your stuff and dumped it out there on the porch and said I should tell you not to be here when he gets back."

Jossie looked up at Kermit and he said, "It's all right. Let's go."

Jossie stood up and put her hand on Rose's shoulder. "Don't carry on like that. It's not your fault."

"I don't care. I feel awful anyway. I told him about the baby and everything but he wouldn't listen." She stopped suddenly. She looked first at Jossie, then at Kermit. Then she dropped her head on her arms and started to cry again.

59

Outside the house, Kermit and Jossie stood facing each other on the sidewalk. "I can't believe it," she said. "I thought you'd be mad."

"Why would I be mad? I think it's great."

He picked up the blanket rolls, put his arms around her waist, and they walked slowly up the street.

"Now I know why you were hinting around this afternoon," he said, "asking all those questions about dogs and alligators."

"I wanted to find out how you felt about it."

"I feel great. I guess I'll turn out to be the world's champion father."

"I wouldn't be surprised," she said.

"Only one thing worries me."

"What's that?"

"What if he looks like you?"

"He wouldn't dare," she said.

"Anything I can't stand, it's an ugly kid. But with my looks and your brains . . ."

"What if he has *my* looks and your brains?"

"We'll throw him back."

"And what if he turns out to be a girl?"

"We'll feed her to the hogs."

They strolled ahead, under the dim street lights, heading toward downtown.

"Have you planned out what we're going to do?" she said.

"Not all of it. That's what I'm chewing over right now. Before you know it, I'll have the whole works laid out."

Half an hour later they sat in a coffee shop on Causey Street, a block east of the bus station, Jossie silent, sipping her coffee, Kermit scribbling figures on a scrap of paper.

"I guess it makes sense," she said. "But why does it have to be Slocum?"

"Because we need a car, and we don't have much money. Slocum's the only place I know where I can get a good car cheap. I was counting on leaving here with more money than we've got. So now we'll have to make do."

"What if that friend of yours isn't there anymore?"

"He'll be there. He's been hustling cars in Slocum since he was sixteen years old. He's a real hot dog. He'll fix me up."

"I still don't see why I can't go with you. Why do I have to go back to Kittredge by myself?"

"You know. Those money orders are there. About eighty dollars left over from the money I sent Mom. And we need it."

"Couldn't Agnes send it to us?"

"How can she? We don't know where we'll be. We can't light anyplace for very long. Besides," he said, "you have to go there and put on your act."

"That's another thing. I'm no good at stuff like that. I don't think I can fool anybody."

"Sure you can. While you're saying it, just pretend it's the truth. If *you* believe it, they'll believe it, too."

"I don't know . . ."

"Well, I know. You can do it."

"Mostly I hate to go by myself."

"I know you do. I hate it too. But that's the only way it will work."

"You sure it'll just be a week?" she said.

"One week from tonight I'll be there. I promise."

They walked over to the bus station. Kermit waited outside while Jossie bought her ticket. Then they stood near the loading gate in the half-light and watched the passengers getting on the bus. Finally the driver said, "Last call, folks," and Kermit walked her to the front of the bus.

"I'm scared," she said.

"You're always scared."

"I hate to go away like this."

"A week from tonight we'll be on our way to Nebraska. Forget everything else and think about that."

She got on the bus. Up the steps and all the way back, till she found a window seat. She watched him through the tinted windows, but he couldn't see her. He waved when the bus pulled out. She could see him standing there, looking for her and waving, but not able to see her.

Part Five

60

Early morning, Jossie sat with Melvin and Agnes in their kitchen, the sun slanting through the window, the room warm from the wood stove and rich with the smells of side meat and sausage, eggs and coffee and oven toast.

"I never would have believed it of him," Agnes said. "It's not like Kermit at all."

"Well, I'm not making it up," Jossie said. "It's not the kind of a story anybody would want to make up."

Agnes walked over from the stove and sat down at the table. "I didn't mean that, honey. But everything's coming at us pretty fast. And it's hard to think of Kermit doing a thing like that."

"Maybe so. But I sure wouldn't be sitting here now if he hadn't."

"Are you sure he didn't know this girl?" Melvin said. "Someplace before, maybe."

Jossie shook her head. "It was just like I told you. We found this little hotel down in Knoxville. Remember, I wrote you from there."

"Said you were headed for Mexico," Agnes said.

"That's right. We were. But we decided to stay off the road for a few days, just hole up and keep out of sight. That's when we met this girl. She worked at a lunch counter right next to the hotel. They had it fixed with a passageway so you could go from the hotel right into the lunch place without going outdoors. And this girl was always there, behind the counter. She seemed kind of sweet and friendly, so we used to talk to her every time we dropped in for a cup of coffee or a sandwich."

"That's all there was to it?" Agnes said. "You mean you didn't have any idea what was going on?"

"Far as I could tell, there *wasn't* anything going on. I don't know yet how they worked it out together. When I think back, it seems like Kermit was with me every minute we were there in Knoxville. Then I woke up one morning and he was gone."

"Didn't he leave a note or anything?"

"Not a word. When I missed him, I thought maybe he'd gone to the store for something or walked into town. But then it got to be late afternoon and I was worried sick, so I asked the hotel man if he'd seen him. The man hated to say anything but finally he told me that Kermit had left in the middle of the night with Doris. That was the girl's name."

"I never heard of such a thing," Agnes said.

"The man heard them talking about Mexico, so that must be where they went. Like Kermit and I were planning to do."

"Sounds to me like he turned into a real son-of-a-bitch."

"That's no way to talk, Melvin, and you know it."

"Well, I don't know what else you'd call it."

"I thought when he came to his senses, he'd come back to get me," Jossie said. "So I waited. The man gave me a job making beds there in the hotel and I stayed as long as I could. But finally I knew I was just making an ass of myself. So I gave up and came back here."

61

In a used-car lot on the corner of Locust and Fourteenth Streets in Slocum, Ed Gates, the owner, gray-haired, tired-looking, and overweight, in a baggy plaid suit, leaned under the hood of a brown Plymouth, head-to-head with Herb May, an angular black man in his thirties, wearing white overalls and a baseball cap.

"What do you think?" Gates said.

"I don't know what to think. I ain't sure it's worth the trouble."

"Never mind the trouble. I'll take the trouble if it's worth the money."

"How much you got in it?"

"Nothing yet. And that's the way I like it. I want it running and out of here before it starts to cost me." He straightened up and stepped back, wiping his hands with a rag. Standing fifteen feet away from him he saw Kermit, the burlap-covered shotgun in one hand, a blanket roll over his shoulder.

"Yes, sir," Gates said. "What can I do for you?"

"I'm looking for a friend of mine named Dick Casper."

"Well, you're a few months late. Dick hasn't been around here since last winter." He turned to his mechanic. "February, wasn't it, he quit?"

"About then."

"Middle of February, I think it was, he left."

"You wouldn't happen to know where he's working now?"

"Far as I know, he's *not* working."

"Then you don't know where I could locate him?"

"He used to live straight across the street there, that house with gray shutters. But he moved out right after the first year. Couldn't say where he lives now."

"He's been moving around, I hear," Herb said.

"Well . . . thanks, anyway."

As Kermit turned away, Herb said, "There's a pool hall on Sycamore Street about ten squares west of here. You might find him there. Ernie's Poolroom it's called."

62

The poolroom was dim and cool, shades closed against the afternoon sun; Ernie, chinless and belligerent, behind the counter, half a dozen men shooting pool, a dozen more dozing or watching from chairs along the wall, and Kermit in a booth by the front window. Dick Casper, a flabby boy his own age, pale skin, freckles, and dark circles under his eyes, was sitting across from him.

"I could have fixed you up good if I was still there."

"That's what I was counting on," Kermit said.

"Be no sweat at all if I was still peddling cars. But I'm not."

"Well, I'll scare up something, I guess. Maybe I'll go back to that lot where you used to work."

"I don't know. If I was you . . . I mean you have to be careful with Gates. He can steal your underwear without even taking your pants down."

"I was hoping you'd come with me. So I don't get stung."

"Not me, buddy. Not with Gates. He and I don't hit it off too good. He thinks everybody's as crooked as he is." Tilting his beer bottle up, Dick took a long, gurgling drink. When he put the bottle down, squinting at Kermit through a cloud of cigarette smoke, he said, "I know of a couple other guys though. I'm pretty well-connected in this town. How much you got to spend?"

"Close to two hundred. But I hate to spend it all."

"Oh, shit, Kermit. You're asking for a miracle. Gates wouldn't give you the sweat off his balls for two hundred."

"I know it's not much. That's why I came looking for you. I figured you could find me something if anybody could."

Dick leaned back in the booth. "Two hundred. Jesus . . ." He took a deep drag on his cigarette. "All right. I'll tell you what. You come and sack in at my place tonight, and tomorrow first thing I'll dig you up some wheels."

"No chance of doing it this afternoon, I guess."

Dick looked up at the clock over the tobacco counter. "No. Afraid not. It's too late already. My buddy gets off work at four. But don't worry about it. I'll put you up, you'll get a good night's sleep, and we'll fix you up bright and early in the morning." He fished a quarter out of his pocket and plunked it on the table. "I'll match you for another beer."

63

Clara Floyd, half-sitting, half-lying on the sofa in the parlor, a thin robe wrapped around her, held a cigarette in one hand, a cup of coffee in the other.

Jossie sat across the room on a straight chair. "I'd have come to see you yesterday," she said, "but I was feeling rotten."

"I heard you were here but I figured if you didn't want to see your mother, that was up to you."

"It wasn't that way, Mom."

"I mean I've done all the running I'm going to do. Anybody that doesn't want to bother with me doesn't have to. I'm through kissing people's asses, I promise you that."

"Oh, Mom, it wasn't like that."

"Then why didn't you come here to stay like you ought to?"

"I just thought I'd spend some time with Melvin and Agnes. They asked me to."

"It looks queer to people. You've got a house here to stay in, with a room of your own, and instead you're up there in that houseful of kids, sleeping on whatever kind of a bed you can find."

"It's just for a few days."

"Does that mean you're going back up to McKeesport?"

"I don't know yet."

"Is your job still waiting for you or not?"

"I guess it is. Theron said it would be. But I have to think about it."

"You've got some thinking to do, all right. If ever I saw a girl make a fool of herself, it was you."

"Yeah, I guess I did."

"I told you he'd never marry you. Didn't I sit right here and tell you that?"

Jossie twined her fingers together in her lap. "You're right, Mom. I should have listened to you."

When she left her mother's house and turned down the street, Jim August's car rolled up quietly, slowed down to her pace, and followed along beside her like a dog at heel.

"I thought maybe I'd be bumping into you," he said. "I heard you came home."

"That's right."

"We all figured you were long gone. Up to New York to get yourself on television. Or out to Hollywood maybe. Sure didn't count on seeing you back here."

"Lay off, Jim. You don't have to make me feel any

dumber than I already do."

"Old Kermit didn't turn out to be such a hero after all, the way I hear it."

"I didn't say he was a hero."

"The way I remember it, you thought he was pretty hot stuff."

"Well, I don't think that now," she said.

"You could have saved yourself a whole lot of trouble, you know, if you'd just listened to me."

"Don't rub it in."

"Next time maybe you'll pay some attention," he said.

She stopped in front of Melvin's garage and Jim stopped with her, smiling through the open car window, the car engine purring and throbbing. She looked at him for a long moment, total mystery in her eyes, no expression to clue her feelings. Then she smiled and said, "Maybe I will."

64

Eleven o'clock at night, on a dark, tree-lined street in Slocum, Kermit and Dick Casper stopped on the sidewalk in front of a gray frame house, trimmed with white, three stories high and a wide veranda on two sides.

"Don't say anything when we get inside," Dick said. "My landlady's a pain in the ass. If she hears anybody talking, she gets the idea I'm running a cathouse upstairs."

They walked up the sidewalk, up the steps, crossed the porch, and let themselves in the front door. They closed it quietly behind them and climbed the stairs.

Dick's room was on the east side of the house, with a wide bay window looking out over the yard. Once a spacious master bedroom, or a second-floor sitting room perhaps, it was now worn and empty-looking, a square of linoleum partly covering the scarred floor, dingy curtains and paper blinds, a narrow bed and a crippled couch, a wooden table, one straight chair, a floor lamp with a small bulb and a battered shade, paint flaking, wallpaper peeling, a rusty sink in one corner with a cracked mirror over it.

After he'd closed the door and switched on the light, Dick said, "We can talk now if we hold it down. The old biddy is usually crapped out by this time." He took a coin out of his pocket. "There's a bed here and a suicide couch over there. I'll flip you for the bed."

"No, you won't. I'll take the couch."

"Never pass anything up when it's offered to you, Kermit. You never know when you'll come up a big winner." He flipped the coin, caught it, and slapped it on the back of his left hand, leaving his right hand over it. "How's about it?" he said.

"All right. Tails."

Dick looked at the coin. "Tails it is. You get the bed."

"Jesus, Dick, I don't want to steal your bed."

"You're not stealing it. You won it. If you'd lost, I'd let you sleep on the floor. I'm looking out for Number One, just like everybody else."

65

Kermit woke up slowly. He turned from his stomach to his side, then rolled over on his back. His eyes fluttered open, closed, then opened again. Head resting on the pillow, he stared up at the unfamiliar ceiling, unsure where he was, feeling the morning air float through the window and across his bed, hearing a vacuum cleaner somewhere downstairs, sensing hunger suddenly as food smells drifted into the room, coffee and frying bacon.

Up on one elbow, he glanced around the room, saw his

bedroll against the wall, his clothes hanging on the back of a chair. And the couch where Dick had slept, a rumpled blanket still covering it. But Dick wasn't there.

Kermit sat up on the edge of the bed, ran a hand through his hair, and rubbed his eyes. He leaned over, picked up his socks, and pulled them on. Walking to the sink, he washed his face and hands, then picked up his pants and put them on. As he tucked in his shirt-tail, his left hand checked the hip pocket where he kept his wallet. Quickly, then, both hands went through all his pockets. Then again. Several times.

He covered the room, searching it, untied his bedroll, pulled back the blankets on the couch, lifted the cushions. Feeling drained and dry, his eyes hot and his hands damp, he was halfway out the door when he looked back and saw the wallet, leaning against the baseboard in the far corner of the room, open, as if it had been tossed there.

He crossed the room and picked it up. His I.D. was there, his driver's license and social security card. Everything except the money. The place where he'd tucked away the thin packet of tens and twenties was empty.

Downstairs, the landlady had switched off her vacuum cleaner. Wearing carpet slippers and a faded kimono, she moved slowly around the room, carrying a dirty rag, damp with water and furniture polish, dusting.

When she heard his knocking, she went quickly to the door. As soon as she pulled it open, Kermit said, "I want to ask you some questions."

"*I'll* ask the questions. How'd you get in here? Ain't nobody but the roomers got keys to the front door."

"Where's Dick Casper?"

"I guess he let you in. Did he?"

"Did you see him go out this morning?"

"I got strict rules about outsiders . . ."

"Wait a minute," Kermit said. "You listen to me because I don't have time to say it twice. I had two hundred dollars stolen from me right here in your house. Now you either settle down and tell me what I need to know about Dick Casper or you're gonna have policemen coming out of your ears."

A few minutes later, he came out the front door, carrying his gear, walking fast. He turned right for two blocks, left for three, then right again. Entering a small coffee shop, dirty windows, flies buzzing, four or five people on stools and a surly counter girl, Kermit spoke to the man in a sweatshirt behind the cash register, keeping his voice steady and even. "I'm a friend of Dick Casper's. His landlady told me he comes here for breakfast sometimes."

"Once in a while," the man said. "But I haven't seen him today." He turned to the waitress. "Dick ain't been in, has he?"

"Not yet. Doubt if he's up yet."

"He's up," Kermit said.

"There's a diner over on Hoover Street. You might try there."

It was half a mile away. When he got there, the counterman, hugely fat, with dark sweat-stains on his shirt and his side-hair combed thin across his bald head, said, "Haven't seen anything of him. Saw him two or three days ago but haven't laid eyes on him since. If I was you, I'd try the Coney Island Grill."

Freshly painted, clean and crowded and a juke-box playing, the Coney Island Grill had a euchre game going in one of the back booths. And a gray-haired woman, thin, with a chicken neck, wearing a red-checked apron and a chef's hat, was behind the counter frying eggs, grilling frankfurters, and pouring coffee. She laughed when she heard Dick's name.

"If you find him, say that Esther asked about him. Tell him I'd like to see that fourteen dollars he owes me. He hasn't set foot in here since I hung that sign up." She pointed to a wall sign, white letters on a red background, that said NO CREDIT. "I've passed him on the street a time or two, but he makes himself scarce in a hurry. Only thing I can tell you is to try the Shamrock Bar. They'll be open shortly. Or else the poolroom. He'll turn up there sooner or later."

At the Shamrock Bar, there were no customers. The bartender sat on a stool, the morning newspaper spread open on the bar in front of him. He didn't look up. "Try the poolroom," he said.

66

It was ten forty in the morning when Kermit found a seat in a dark corner at the back of Ernie's poolroom. He sat there, not leaving his chair, till after four in the afternoon, eyes on the front door.

Finally, nearly four thirty, when he'd invented and discarded a whole list of hopeless alternatives, when he'd starved himself dizzy rather than spend any of the few dollars still in his pocket, he saw Dick stroll through the front door, jacket open, hands in his pockets, loose and easy, joking with the man behind the cigar counter.

"How they ridin', Orville?" His voice floated back across the pool tables, the click of balls, and the uneven drone of separate conversations.

"About six and six," Orville said. "How's yourself?"

"Moving around," Dick said. "Keeping the left up. Hat nailed on and a tight ass-hole." He shook out a cigarette, lit it, and swung back through the room, cuffing and goosing his cronies as he cruised along, heading for the toilet. Riding high and full of himself, a wide smile on his face, he swaggered past where Kermit was sitting and on through the doorway marked HOMBRES. Bellying up to the urinal, he unzipped himself, groaned, and said, "Ohhh . . . Jesus." He directed a steady stream toward the screen-wire at the bottom, clogged with cigar stumps and cigarette butts. He sang softly to himself, looking down with full concentration, admiring himself and the incomparable act he was performing. Finally he shook himself elaborately, tucked his toy away, zipped up his pants, and turned around.

Kermit stood five feet away, his back against the rest room door. "All right, you son-of-a-bitch, where's my money?"

Dick's face quivered with a strange expression, some hint that the punishment if it came might give him more pleasure than the crime had. He licked his lips, smiled a wet smile, and said, "I'm not gonna lie to you, Kermit. I took it."

"I know damned well you took it. And I want it back. Right now."

"I wish I could accommodate you."

"Don't give me any bullshit."

"I mean I wish I could give it to you. But I can't."

"Cut the crap, Dick."

"I mean it. I'm leveling with you. I just plain haven't got it."

"Then you'd better just plain go and *get* it."

"Look, Kermit . . . I had a debt. A real ball-breaker. I mean I was into somebody for two hundred, a little over, and I had to cough it up. No fucking around. I had to pay it."

Kermit grabbed him by the front of his shirt. "Not with *my* money, you didn't."

"I was scared, Kermit. I was scared shitless. These are mean guys. Out-of-town. They were gonna mash me like a potato."

"What do you think *I'm* gonna do?" Kermit shoved him against the wall with a thump, pulled him back, then rapped him against the wall again.

Dick hung limp and soft, without bones or muscle, no tension, no resistance, eyes round and empty, a rag doll. "I don't blame you," he said. "I deserve it. It was a crummy thing to do."

Kermit drove him against the wall again, harder this time. "That wasn't your money, you bastard. I worked my ass off for that money. I *need* it."

"They were dogging me. They were right on my ass. I didn't want to take it from you, but I was scared."

"Where are these guys, the ones you gave the money to?"

"They're long gone. Took off at eight this morning. I told you, they're out-of-towners. Steubenville, Pittsburgh, they move around."

Kermit stared at him, holding him hard against the wall. Then, suddenly, he dropped him. Dick sagged and stumbled, lurched against the urinal, and almost fell.

"You can see what kind of a crack I was in." He straightened himself up, studying Kermit closely, watching his eyes. "But I promise you one thing. I'll make it up to you. I'll square this with you if it's the last thing I do."

Kermit looked at him for a long moment. "Yeah. Sure you will." He turned and went out the door, picked up his gear in the corner where he'd left it and walked the length of the room to the front door.

Outside, he looked both ways, up and down the street. Then he started to his right, moving slowly. He walked without stopping for more than an hour, till the sun had cooled and long shadows striped the streets and sidewalks from the west.

He turned into a coffee shop and had a cup of coffee and a refill, pouring in a lot of milk and sugar to dull his hunger. After he paid the waitress he counted his money. Four dollars and eighty-seven cents.

On a high street overlooking the town he found a bench. He sat there listening to the traffic sounds and trying to find answers to the questions that sling-shotted through his head.

Finally, the evening cooling off around him, lights switching on all over the city, he made a choice. He got up from the bench and walked five blocks downhill to a supermarket, spot lights on the building, banks of white lights on poles circling the parking lot.

He wandered through the lines of parked cars, aimless, it seemed, loose and easy, till he saw what he was looking for. Through the rolled-down window of a red Chevrolet, he saw a set of keys dangling from the ignition. He opened the door on the driver's side, tossed his gear across the front seat, and slid in under the steering wheel.

When he pulled out of the parking lot, he turned right and drove carefully through residential streets, observing all signs and speed limits, till he saw a sign for Highway 119. At the intersection, he turned left and headed northeast out of town.

Part Six

67

"I don't care what happens to him," Jossie said. She was sitting in an office at the state police barracks just outside Buckhannon. Lieutenant Bardy, behind a steel desk facing her, and Les Klauser, a husky, light-haired man in an army uniform, captain's rank, in a chair beside the desk, also facing her.

"He ditched me and I don't owe him anything," she went on. "But I'm not going to lie about him. He didn't hit Chet. I'll swear to that. It happened just the way I told you. Chet was out in the yard kidding around with those two M.P.'s, and all of a sudden they got into a scuffle and one of them cracked him over the head with a billy club. Kermit wasn't even outdoors when it happened. He and I were watching through the kitchen window."

Bardy studied her for a moment, tapping his pencil on the desk. Then he turned to Klauser and said, "You have any more questions, Captain?"

"No. I think we covered it."

"All right." Bardy turned back to Jossie. "Captain Klauser will take your statement back to Camp Eustis with him and I'll file a copy here. What you've told us might change the whole picture. We may have to ask a lot more questions than we figured on."

Jossie stood up. "Does that mean I have to stay in Kittredge?"

"We're not going to detain you if that's what you mean. But if you go somewhere, we'll need to know how we can reach you."

"My mother's in Kittredge," she said. "She'll always know where I am."

After she'd left the room, Bardy said, "What do you think?"

"You never know. But she seems straight to me. I'll have a better idea about it after I put the squeeze on Roach and Meeker."

"What about Docker?"

"I feel sorry for the poor bastard. If what the girl says is true, he's running for nothing."

"You think he's in Mexico."

"I'd bet my pension on it."

Outside the building, Jossie walked across the driveway and got into Jim August's car. "How'd it go?"

"I told them the truth," she said.

He sat there without starting the car and said, "You're still sore at me, aren't you?"

"Why should I be sore at you, just because you dragged me over here and got me questioned for two hours like I was some kind of a crook?"

"That's my job, for Christ's sake."

"That's what I mean," she said. "You've got a crappy job."

"They been looking for you and Kermit ever since you took off. I couldn't pretend I didn't see you."

"Let's go. I gotta get back."

"You're mad as hell, aren't you?"

"No. I'm not mad."

"You sure?"

"Yes, I'm sure."

"Good. That's more like it." He started the car, pulled out on the highway, and turned southeast toward Kittredge. He drove fast and they didn't talk. But after he angled off the pavement and took the gravel road cutting across to Beverly, he said, "I still can't dope it out."

"What's that?

"Why Kermit would take off with somebody else when he could have you."

"I thought we weren't going to talk about that anymore."

"I'm not trying to make you feel bad . . ."

"Then don't talk about it."

". . . but it really is something I can't figure." He waited for an answer but he didn't get one. "What kind of a girl was she anyway?"

"I told you twenty times. She was a waitress."

"I mean what did she look like?"

"I told you that, too."

"I know you did. But I can't make it fit. It doesn't make any sense to me."

Jossie went slowly, trying to remember what she'd said before, anxious not to contradict herself. "Like I said she was an ordinary, everyday girl. Not very tall. A thin face. Long brown hair and big eyes. Nothing special to look at."

"He must have gone off his nut. That's all *I* can figure." As they turned into Kittredge, Jim said, "How would you like to drive up to Elkins tonight?"

"I don't think so. Not tonight."

"Why not? It's as good a night as any."

"Let me catch my breath first. I've only been home here since Tuesday."

"Same old stuff. Right?"

"I just need a few days to get hold of myself."

"You know something. Ever since I transferred in here, I've been getting the business from you. First up in Dunstan. Now here. The same old stall."

"It's not a stall," she said. "Before, I told you I wouldn't go out with you at all. Now I'm saying I will."

He pulled up in front of Melvin's garage and stopped, leaving the motor running. "What I want to know is *when.*"

She got out of the car, walked around the front to the driver's side. As he leaned out through the open window and started to say something, she bent down quickly and kissed him on the mouth. "Don't get yourself in an uproar," she said. "Everything's going to be all right." She turned and walked across the sidewalk, up the outside stairs, and into the house.

68

At a Mobil station on the highway just east of Ivydale, Kermit sat behind the wheel and watched the attendant rack up the nozzle, then walk around to him, wiping his hands with a rag. "That'll be two dollars and thirty cents."

Kermit took a crumpled bill and some change out of his pocket and counted it out in the man's palm. What was left, a dime, a nickel, and three pennies, he put back in his pocket.

A mile up the highway he veered off onto a dirt road. At the first wide spot he turned around and parked under the trees, half a mile off the highway. He sat there for two hours, staring straight ahead through the windshield, one hand feeling the coins in his pocket, the other resting on the shotgun beside him on the front seat.

It was dusk when he started the car, drove back to the highway, and turned northeast toward Bock nine miles away. At a liquor store on the edge of town, he pulled in and parked. He got out of the car carrying a brown paper shopping bag and went into the store. A skinny white-haired man was behind the counter, rimless glasses and false teeth that didn't fit. "Evening," he said.

"Evening."

"What can I do for you?"

Kermit put the shopping bag on the counter, keeping one hand out of sight inside it. "I've got a shotgun in this bag," he said. "It's pointing directly at your stomach." The old man took a step backward and Kermit said, "Don't get jumpy now. Don't move around."

"What do you want?"

"Mostly I don't want you to make me nervous. This is the first time I ever held anybody up and I want to be sure I get it right." He looked at the cash register. "Now here's what you do. Just hoist yourself up a little and stretch out, belly-down, across this counter. I want to see your arms hanging down on one side and your legs on the other."

The old man bent over, hitched himself up, and draped limp across the counter.

"That's good," Kermit said. "Now just stay there for a while."

Watching the old man, he backed around the end of the counter to the register, opened it, and dumped the bills and coins into his shopping bag. Crab-walking to the door then, still watching the old man, he opened it and ran to his car.

Twenty minutes later he pulled into a one-pump Gulf station between Servia and Elmira. The owner was coop-erative. He stayed outside on the driveway, sitting on his hands, while Kermit emptied the cash drawer into his bag.

Six miles farther north he found a country grocery store just closing for the day. When he explained about the shotgun, they gave him eighteen dollars out of the money box. Kermit picked out seven dollars and ninety-four cents' worth of groceries then and paid cash for them.

An hour later, he drove into the outskirts of Feeney, found a supermarket and parked his car there. He strolled through the lanes of cars as he had in Slocum till he found one with the keys in the ignition, a blue Ford. He tossed his gear into the front seat and drove due east out of town till he found a north-bound gravel road. Ten miles on that, three miles on a dirt road, then he turned off into a patch of woods, parked in a grove of young beech trees, crawled into the back seat, and went to sleep.

Next morning when he woke up, he washed himself in a stream, ate a cold breakfast, and sat in the car till noon listening to the radio. He ate a sandwich and drank a cola he'd cooled in the stream. Then he drove north through Cedarville and on up to Cedar Creek State Park.

He spent the afternoon there, hiking the trails and studying the road map he carried in his jacket pocket.

That evening, at nine thirty, he was standing in a liquor store at the west edge of Glenville, a tough, stringy old woman glaring at him from behind the counter.

"I don't care what you say, I'm not giving in," she said. "I don't have but thirty dollars in that register and I need it just as much as you do. Maybe more."

"You see this shotgun, don't you?"

"I see it all right. But you're not about to shoot a person for any thirty dollars. At least I don't think you are. I've seen a lot of mean guys. You're not one of them."

"What if you're wrong?"

"Then I'll be dead, I guess. Unless you're a bad shot."

Kermit couldn't keep from smiling. "Look," he said.

"Why don't you just hand over ten bucks and we'll call it square?"

"I'm not going to do that either. You drove up in a nice car out there and I have to walk to work. What's fair about that?"

"You're making it awful hard for me to earn a living."

"I'm not worried about you. You'll have better luck down the road a ways."

Twenty minutes later, Kermit pulled into a filling station on Highway 5, seven miles southeast of Glenville. A red-haired man in a Mickey Mouse sweatshirt and a straw hat trotted out to the pumps. "Yes, sir."

"Fill it up. High-test. You got a Coke machine inside?"

"Right inside the door. You can't miss it."

Kermit got out of the car and walked into the station office. The operator, serene and prosperous, owner of his own business, two bright children, an obliging wife, and sixty acres down the road, sang softly to himself as he checked the oil and tires, filled the radiator, cleaned the windshield, wiped off the hood, and re-racked the gas hose.

Still singing, he walked across the drive and into his office. Kermit was leaning against the soft drink machine, a half-empty bottle in his hand.

"You're all set," the man said. "That'll be seven sixty-five." Kermit handed him a ten-dollar bill and he rang open the cash register. He stood there staring at the empty money drawer. When he turned to look at Kermit, he saw the twin barrels of the shotgun nosing out through the burlap wrapping. Checking the register again, not believing what he saw, he looked back at Kermit. "You . . ."

Kermit nodded his head and said, "That's right." He stepped forward and plucked the ten-dollar bill out of the man's hand. Just before he backed across the driveway to his car he said, "You ought to get yourself some decent clothes. You look like an ass-hole in that shirt."

69

Jim August, a cigarette tucked in the corner of his mouth, his right arm extended across the back of the car seat, turned east out of Kittredge on the road leading to Glade, driving smoothly, the rear-view mirror cocked so he could glance up and see himself, the sun shining warm through the windshield, the police radio quiet except for occasional ripples of static.

A mile or so outside Kittredge he turned into the front yard of a country church, white-washed and well-tended, a polished bell in the open tower, a proper roof, and grass cut close all around.

Jossie, on a knoll behind the church, in the stone-fenced cemetery plot, beside Chet's grave, kneeling down to secure a vase of wildflowers in the fresh dirt, looked up and saw Jim get out of his car.

As he walked across the churchyard toward the cemetery, out of ear-shot of his two-way radio, it buzzed and popped and crackled sharply to life.

"Attention, all units. Be on the watch for a 1972 blue Ford sedan, West Virginia license 362–2164. Driver is a white male, early twenties, wanted for questioning about two armed robberies last night between Glenville and Weston. Proceed with caution. Suspect is armed with a shotgun and should be considered dangerous."

Strolling across the graveyard toward Jossie, Jim said, "You mean to say you *walked* all the way out here?"

"It's not so far."

"I'd have chauffeured you here in no time if you'd just said the word."

"That's nice of you. But I didn't mind the walk. I like

to look at the leaves turning and watch the squirrels getting ready for winter."

"Haven't seen much of you," he said. "Thought maybe you disappeared again."

"I've been right there at Melvin's."

"Not yesterday you weren't."

"No, that's right, I wasn't," Jennie said. "My girl friend from Dunstan came down to pick me up. We drove over to Cassity to visit with her folks."

"You must have got home pretty late."

"No, we didn't. I was back before dark."

"That's funny. I drove past Melvin's at nine thirty or so and there wasn't a light anywhere."

"I was in bed, I expect. Melvin and Agnes drove down to Huttonsville to see his uncle and I stayed with the kids. Soon as I got them to bed, I went to sleep myself."

"What are you turning into? An old lady?"

"I guess so."

When Jossie finished her work, they walked to the car and got in. The radio started to crackle again and Jim snapped it off.

"You're not supposed to do that, are you?" Jossie said. "What if there's a crime wave all of a sudden?"

"Then they'll have to handle it without me."

He backed the car out to the road and headed down the hill toward Kittredge.

"When I couldn't locate you last night, I drove over to Elkins. Stopped in at Gephart's place for a drink. You ever been there?"

"I guess I was. A year or so ago. It's too crazy for me."

"I know what you mean. But it's calmed down now. They got a couple guys playing guitars and you can get a pretty good steak for the money." He looked at her. "I thought you and I might cruise up there tonight and have a little fun."

"Well, that's not such a bad idea, I guess . . ."

"Whatever you're getting warmed up to say, I don't want to hear it."

"I didn't even finish."

"I know you didn't and I don't want you to. You've been back here for close to a week now and every time I see you I get a different kind of a no. If you're still hung up with that boyfriend of yours, why don't you come out and say so?"

"I'm not. I told you that."

"Then what's the problem?"

"I don't feel good. *That's* the problem. I've been feeling lousy all week long."

"You look healthy to me."

"I didn't mean that. I don't need a doctor or anything. It's just . . . God, you men are so dumb." When he looked at her, she said, "I've got cramps, you dope. Is that plain enough? All I feel like doing is staying in bed with a hot water bottle."

"Well, I'm sorry. I mean I'm no mind-reader. You should have said something."

"Don't worry about it. I'll be good as new in a couple days. Then we'll drive over to Elkins and make up for lost time."

Jim slowed down for the turn into Kittredge, grinned at her and said, "Lady, you just made yourself a deal."

70

In a patch of deep woods southwest of Horner, Kermit sat in the front seat of his car, both front doors open, late-morning sun slanting down through the trees, counting the money in his wallet and listening to the radio.

". . . and that makes a total of eight hold-ups in the last six days."

Kermit turned the volume up.

"Police believe the same man is responsible for all the robberies. He carries a shotgun wrapped in sacking and was last seen driving a blue Ford sedan."

Kermit clicked the radio off, got out of the car, and moved around it slowly, looking it over. Finally he walked to the creek bank nearby, dug out a double handful of wet clay, and smeared it on the hood of the car. It dried quickly in the sun, leaving the shiny blue metal with a dull brown coating. Kermit studied the effect, then walked back to the creek for more clay.

Late that afternoon, nearly dusk, he pulled out of the woods where he'd spent the day, bumped along on a dirt road for two miles, turned onto a paved road, and headed east.

Eight miles past Buckhannon, he pulled into a Shell station, stopped by the pumps, and got out. A tall bony kid, eighteen or so, wearing glasses, a red shirt, and greasy jeans, came ambling out.

"Fill it up," Kermit said, "and check the oil."

"Right." Matter-of-fact and cocky, the easy security of a man who knows engines and nothing else.

"Where's the can?" Kermit said.

"Around the corner there. Key's inside the front door on your right."

The kid busied himself with the car as Kermit stepped into the office, picked up the key, and disappeared behind the garage. In a moment he was back. He stopped at the corner of the building and shouted at the kid. "What the hell kind of a joint is this anyway?" The kid straightened up and looked at him. "Come here a minute," Kermit said. "I want to show you something."

"What's the matter?"

"What's the *matter?* Come here and I'll show you." As the kid walked toward him, Kermit said, "I've been in some crummy places but this is the worst."

"What's wrong?"

"What's *wrong?* There's a dead cat in there."

"A what?"

"A dead cat, for Christ's sake. Right in the toilet."

"There ain't either. I just checked in there a while ago."

"You calling me a liar, kid?"

"No, I didn't mean that."

"Just take a look for yourself," Kermit said. He led the way to the door, then stepped back so the kid could go in first. As soon as he was inside, Kermit pulled the door shut and locked it from the outside.

Inside, as the door slammed and locked, the kid turned back quickly and tried the knob. "Hey, what are you doing?"

Through the door, he heard Kermit's voice. "Don't make any racket in there or I'll unhook the pumps and let all your gas run out."

As he walked away toward his car, he heard the kid's voice, muffled, through the door. "Hey, there's no dead cat in here!"

Kermit drove the Ford around to the back of the garage, steered slowly across the rough lot, littered with trash and car parts, all the way back to the lip of a deep ravine. He got out of the car with his shotgun and blanket roll and dropped them on the ground. Then he put the car in gear, pushed it down a short incline, and over the edge into the ravine. It bumped and squeaked, rolled twice, end-over, and disappeared into a heavy thicket at the bottom of the slope.

Kermit walked back to the station office, emptied the cash register into his pockets, put on a paper cap with SHELL printed on it, and sat by the front door on a box waiting for a customer to pull in.

After a dozen cars drove by, one turned into the driveway and stopped, not by the pumps, but directly in front of the office, where Kermit was sitting. It was a state police car, a middle-aged trooper with thick sideburns and a moustache squeezed in behind the wheel.

Kermit walked over to the car. "How's it going?"

"Not much excitement," the trooper said. "I got kinda thirsty. Thought maybe I'd bum a Coke off you guys."

"Coming up." Kermit went inside to the soft drink machine and came back quickly with an opened bottle.

"Thanks," the trooper said. "Just what I needed." He took a long swig and looked around, "Where's Arnie?"

"Arnie? Oh . . . he got hungry. Went off to get himself a meal."

"Jesus, he must be in the money. Usually he brings something in a paper bag that his mother fixed." He tilted the bottle up again and emptied it.

"Want another one?" Kermit said.

"Better not. I'll be belching my socks up as it is." A deep growl came up out of his chest. "You see what I mean?" He started his engine. "Don't think I ever saw you around before. You been working here long?"

Kermit shook his head. "I don't work here at all. I'm Arnie's cousin from over at Harrisonburg. Just here for a visit."

"Yeah . . . well, when Arnie gets back tell him there's some cowboy with a shotgun been sticking up filling stations right and left. Driving a blue Ford. Tell him to keep his eyes peeled."

"I'll do that." Kermit stood with his hands in his pockets watching the police car pull away in the dark and disappear up the road. Then he walked behind the building on the side opposite the men's toilet.

He waited there, out of sight, till he heard another car turn in and stop by the gas pumps. A horn honked but Kermit stayed where he was. The horn sounded again. Then he heard a car door open and slam, footsteps on the concrete, and a man's voice, husky and impatient,

"Where the hell *is* everybody? Come on! I need some gas."

Kermit trotted out from behind the building then. A pot-bellied man in a safety helmet turned toward him, canvas jacket, corduroy pants, and laced-up construction workers' shoes. Before he could say anything, Kermit rushed up to him. "Boy, am I glad to see you. I need somebody to give me a hand."

"I'm in a hurry, kid."

"This'll just take a minute."

"I ain't *got* a minute. I need five gallons of regular . . ."

"You got to help me. There's a woman having a baby . . ."

"There's a what?"

". . . in there." Kermit said, pointing toward the building.

"In where?"

"Right in there. Around the corner. In the women's can." Kermit took him by the arm and guided him toward the building.

"Now, wait a minute. I'm no doctor. I don't know . . ."

"It's all right. I just need somebody to help *lift* her. She's a big woman and she's got herself in an awkward position. It'll just take us a minute."

"What you ought to do is call a doctor."

"I did. He's on his way here now."

The door of the women's toilet was half open. "Right in there," Kermit said. He held the door back so the other man could go through, then pulled it shut quickly and locked it from the outside. He tossed the key into the bushes and walked back to the gas pumps. While the tank of the pickup truck was filling up, he got his gear from the office and put it in the front seat. As he drove out on the road, he could hear the two men behind him, yelling and pounding on the doors.

71

Jim August walked into the cool of Melvin's garage, late afternoon of a gray, misty day, the sky blowing clear now for the first time since morning.

"What kind of a day you call this?"

Melvin looked up from his vise, where he was working on a piece of angle iron with a rough file.

"I don't know what to call it. How about you? How you doing?"

"Good shape. Just finished a plate of ham and eggs and it set me up fine."

"Kinda late for breakfast, ain't it?"

"It wasn't breakfast. More like an early supper. Ham and eggs is something I could eat half a dozen times a day."

"Not me. Can't handle the greasy stuff anymore. I get a knot in my chest like somebody grabbed me with a pliers."

"Sounds like nerves," Jim said.

"No, it's not that. I just can't take too much greasy food."

"I know what you mean. We got a guy over at the barracks can't eat eggs or sausage or anything fried. Can't drink milk either. No cream in his coffee. No pie or cake or butter on his bread."

"What's he live on?"

"Damned if I know. Eats a lot of oatmeal, he says. And he keeps a box of crackers in the glove compartment of his car. Always chewing on crackers."

"Jesus, I'd starve to death if I had to do that. If I had to eat like a bird I'd just as soon grow feathers and turn into one."

"They say most of it's nerves though," Jim said.

"Not me. I never been nervous in my life."

"You chew your fingernails a lot I notice."

"That's not because I'm nervous. It's just a habit I got into when I was a kid."

Jim picked a cigarette out of his shirt pocket with two fingers, positioned it just right in his mouth, and lit it. He took off his wide-brimmed hat and ran one hand through his hair. "Is Jossie around?" he said.

"I guess she's in the house somewhere."

"How's she feeling?"

"Not so hot, Agnes says. Stays to herself a good deal of the time."

Just then, in a bedroom upstairs, Jossie, in her slip, was folding pieces of clothing and packing them, one by one, in a small bag, humming softly to herself.

She picked up a pencil and went to a calendar hanging on the wall over the bed. Six days in a row had been crossed out. Around the seventh day she drew a circle. As she put the pencil back on the dresser, Agnes called up from the kitchen. "Jossie . . . you still up there?"

"Yes."

"Jim August just came in. He wants to see you."

Jossie hesitated. Then, "I can't come down right now. I'm in bed." She closed her bag quickly and shoved it out of sight under the bed.

Downstairs, Agnes turned from the foot of the stairs to Jim August, standing just inside the kitchen door with his hat in his hand. "You heard her," Agnes said. "She's been feeling pretty punk since she came back. Can't seem to get any pep at all."

"I know. That's what she told me." He walked over to the stairs. "But if it's all the same to you, I'd like to run up and see her for a minute."

"Well, I don't know . . ."

"It's all right," he said, starting up the stairs. "I'll just stick my nose in and say hello." Up the steps, two at a time, he tapped on the door at the top.

"It's me, Jim August."

"Oh . . . all right, come on in." Her voice sounded small through the door. He opened it and stepped in. She was in bed with the quilt pulled up over her.

"I just came up to see how you're feeling."

"Well, that's nice of you, but I don't think Melvin's going to like it. It doesn't look right."

"Don't worry about that. I say there's nothing wrong with calling on a sick lady." He sat down on the edge of the bed.

"Are you really sick or just trying to get out of K.P.?"

"It's what I told you before. But I'll be fine in a day or so."

"Anything I can get for you?"

"No, thanks. I don't need a thing."

He glanced up at the calendar. "What's that all about?"

"Nothing. Just crossing off the days."

"I see you made a circle around today. What's that for?" When she didn't answer he said, "Come on. What's the mystery?"

Fishing for an answer, she said, "Don't be nosy now. It's just something personal."

"You have a lot of secrets, don't you?"

"No, it's not that. I just . . ." An answer came to her then. "You re no fun. You have to know everything. I put that circle there because I thought we might be going up to Elkins tonight. I thought I'd be feeling all right today. But I guessed wrong."

"Maybe you'll be better when the sun goes down."

"I don't think so. I'd rather wait till tomorrow if it's all right with you. Tomorrow night we'll go, no matter what."

"Is that a promise?"

"Cross my heart."

72

Off a side road twenty miles east of Buckhannon, in a cluster of pine trees by a deserted gravel pit, Kermit sat in the pickup truck watching the light fade through the trees, waiting for full dark.

He looked at his watch, got out of the truck, and walked to the edge of the pit. Picking up a handful of stones, he threw them, one by one, across to the far edge. Then he walked slowly toward the car, passing under the trees, kicking pine cones ahead of him on the ground.

Inside the truck again, he switched on the radio and slouched down, with his head resting on the back of the seat, listening.

". . . so that's the way it is, mother. If you're looking for an all-purpose flour that's *really* all-purpose . . ."

Twenty-five miles away, Agnes had her kitchen radio turned to the same station.

". . . then you switch to Dunbar's, the flour that's milled in the South for Southern cooks. Now from W-O-L-K in Elkins, here's Porter Waggoner with his big new one, 'Walking to Memphis.' "

Melvin put his coffee cup down and said, "A guy like that is trouble. That's what I mean. He's a state cop and that's bad enough. But on top of it he thinks every woman in the county's got hot pants for him. Wouldn't surprise me if he made a grab for you next. I just don't like him hanging around."

Agnes looked toward the stairs. "Don't talk so loud. She'll hear you."

"I don't care. If she doesn't catch on pretty quick, I'm aiming to tell her. Right out."

"It's not her fault. She doesn't want him hanging around any more than you do."

"How do you know that?"

"I just know. She can't stand him. I think that's why she stays upstairs so much. So she can keep away from him."

"How can she keep away from him if he marches right up to her room like he did today?"

Upstairs, Jossie put on a sweater, picked up her suitcase, and eased the door open. She listened, heard the sound of the radio, the television set in the next room, and Melvin and Agnes talking in the kitchen.

Stepping into the hall, she pulled the door shut behind her and ran quickly to the front stairs. She tiptoed down the steps, crossed the parlor, and let herself out the side door.

In the kitchen, Melvin said, "Nothing's about to stop a bird dog like him. The more she keeps away from him, the more he'll chase her."

"Well, we can afford to wait a day or so before we say anything. She's been talking about maybe going up to Chicago to see her dad."

"The sooner the better. I like her, but she's trouble. Some people are like that. Nothing but trouble, everyplace they go."

It was dark outside now. Jossie ran quickly through the streets to the edge of town, then turned up the narrow road leading to the Docker place.

73

Thirty-five miles away, on the road to Grafton, Jim August cruised north, putting in extra hours, smiling to himself, listing his virtues. He lit a cigarette and half-listened to his radio as it crackled to life.

". . . last reported driving a Dodge pickup truck, orange in color. West Virginia license 387–5642. Driver is believed to be the shotgun bandit who's been moving east from Slocum since a week ago. Latest reports indicate he may be in the Elkins area . . ."

Jim came into focus, reached out and turned up the volume. ". . . suspect is described as a male Caucasian, early twenties, five feet ten inches tall, weighing one hundred and fifty pounds. He is armed with a shotgun. Considered dangerous. Proceed with caution . . ."

August kept driving north, eyes thoughtful, his forehead furrowed, the ash burning long on his cigarette. Suddenly, he checked his rear-view mirror, screeched the car around in a tight U-turn, and headed south toward Kittredge.

74

Minutes after Kermit drove out of the woods and headed east toward Elkins, he came around a curve and saw a car blocking the road, a man standing on the center line signaling with his arms. No room on the narrow road to swing past, Kermit stepped on the brakes and slid to a stop just behind the other car.

As the man walked toward him, Kermit's hand dropped down to the seat and rested on the shotgun.

"My name's Carl Brewster and I got myself a problem. Could you give me a hand?" Short and square, wearing a light-colored suit, a bright tie, and a black soft hat. Shell-rimmed glasses and a pasted-on smile.

"What's the trouble?" Kermit said.

"My car quit on me. Brand new. Not even broken in good. But she quit dead. You know anything about motors?"

"A little bit." Kermit got out of the truck, walked ahead to the car, and lifted up the hood. While Brewster held a flashlight, he searched and tested and tightened things with his fingers, checking wires and connections.

From the front seat of the car a young woman in her thirties with pale blonde hair, wearing a tight dress, pink lipstick, pink nail polish, and green eye-shadow, sat watching through the windshield. Brewster came to the window on the driver's side and leaned in. "He says it looks like a wire shook loose. He's fixing it now. We'll be on our way in a minute or so."

"Boy, you're really something," the girl said.

"What does that mean?"

"I mean you're a real prize. I think maybe I'll send your wife a sympathy card."

"Shut up, damn it. He'll hear you." He stepped back as Kermit moved up beside him.

"Let me give it a try." He opened the door and slid in behind the wheel. As soon as he turned the ignition key, the engine came to life, smooth and powerful. "There you are," he said to the girl. He left the motor running and got out.

"Thanks a lot," Brewster said. "I appreciate it. How much do I owe you?"

"No charge. Glad I could help you." Kermit stepped back and looked at the car. "Sure is a nice automobile. Smells like it's fresh out of the factory."

"Just about. I've got the Chrysler dealership over in Weston. Always drive a new car. Break one in a little, then I sell it and pick myself out another one."

"Well, that's a good deal," Kermit said. Then, "Say, would you mind coming over here to the truck for a second? You know about cars. There's something I want to show you." Brewster followed him to the truck. Kermit reached in, took the shotgun off the seat, and turned around.

"Here's what I wanted to show you. It's a shotgun."

"Yeah, I see it is. Why you got it wrapped up like that?" As the gun barrel came up and touched his belt buckle, Brewster said, "Hey, now wait a minute. What the hell are you doing?"

"You say you're a car trader. I want to swap."

A few minutes later, the orange pickup truck headed back the way it had come, toward Buckhannon, Brewster driving, the girl sitting beside him.

"Jesus," she said. "You really are something."

"Just shut your mouth about it."

"Big car dealer. Don't know an engine from an electric fan. That was a great deal you made back there."

"You saw that shotgun, didn't you?"

"All I saw was you shaking." The girl started to laugh. "I thought you'd shake right out of your pants."

"All right. That's enough out of you. You're finished."

"What does that mean?"

"I mean, my God, I've had enough," he said.

"You've had enough?"

"You're damned right I have. You and that mouth of yours. You're *fired.*" He looked over at her. She was smiling. "What's so God-damned funny? I mean it. You're *fired.*"

The girl pushed her hair back from her face. "That'll be the day. That will *really* be the day."

75

"She must be asleep," Agnes said. "I haven't heard a sound from her since supper." She was holding the baby, patting her, trying to stop her from crying, standing in the doorway between the kitchen and the parlor, Melvin beside her, Jim August facing them from the center of the kitchen.

"You sure she's up there?" he said.

"I don't know where else she'd be. She went up right after we ate."

"I don't like people barging in like this," Melvin said, "slamming doors and waking up the kids. What you and Jossie do is none of my affair, but . . ."

"I'm not making a social call, Melvin. This is police business. And I want to know, once and for all, if she's upstairs in that room or not."

Agnes looked at Melvin. Then she said, "I'll go up and look if it will make you feel any better. But I guarantee you she's there."

Going up the back stairs from the kitchen, Agnes knocked on Jossie's door, waited a moment, and eased it open. The bed lamp was on, but the bed was empty. There was a note pinned to the pillow. Agnes picked it up and read it. Then she slipped it into her apron pocket and went back downstairs.

"Is she there?" Jim said.

"Yes. She's . . . she's sound asleep."

"Are you sure?"

Agnes looked at Melvin and didn't answer.

"I think I'd better take a look for myself," Jim said. He crossed the room and ran up the stairs. Agnes moved quickly to Melvin, handed him the note, and whispered, "She's not there. She left this."

Melvin read the note. "Why'd you lie to him?"

"I didn't know what to say. We'd already told him she was up there."

A door slammed upstairs and Jim came back down to the kitchen. Slowly now. Deliberate steps on the stairs. "All right," he said. "Let's start over."

Melvin handed him the note. "Agnes found this when she went upstairs just now."

Jim took it, unfolded it, read it out loud. "I'm going to Chicago to see Dad. I'll write you from there. Thanks for everything. Jossie."

"It's news to us," Agnes said quickly. "She said she might go there sometime, but she never said when."

"Was she here at supper time? Or did you make that up, too?"

"You saw her yourself late this afternoon," Melvin said.

"I said supper time."

"Yeah. She was here. She ate with us."

"She'd have to go to Elkins to catch the Chicago bus. How'd she get there?"

"*I* didn't take her," Melvin said. "If that's what you're getting at."

"Maybe that girl friend of hers from Dunstan picked her up," Agnes said. "The one she used to work with."

"Or maybe she grew wings and flew." Jim turned and slammed out. They heard his feet running on the gravel; his car engine started, and he drove away.

76

Inside the Docker house, a percolator bubbling on the stove, fruit on the table, sandwiches wrapped in foil, and fresh-cut forest flowers in a glass jar, Jossie picked up the kerosene lamp and walked from the kitchen, through the parlor, to the downstairs bedroom.

Putting the lamp on top of the bureau, she opened the second drawer, rummaged through some folded clothing, and brought out an envelope. She tore it open and took out a packet of paper money with a rubberband around it.

Closing the drawer, she walked back to the kitchen, opened her suitcase, and put the money inside. Then she poured herself a cup of coffee, turned the lamp low, and pulled a chair close to the window so she could look out across the side yard.

It was a clear night. Stars above the ridge line, a few fast clouds scudding across the moon, the headstones in the burial ground clear and silhouetted in the half-dark.

Sliding the window up a few inches, she felt the crisp air against her throat, heard the frogs by the stream behind the house, and the night birds.

And somehow, her head crowded with images and memories, ideas and pictures, familiar things tangled together with things she'd never seen, excited and happy and afraid all in the same moment, it seemed to her she could hear isolated, echoing notes and tones and chords from Chet's guitar, not connected to each other or to anything else, just floating through the gauzy fabric of sounds and sights and smells that surrounded her there.

𝄢

Kermit drove down the narrow back road that bypassed Kittredge, the route he and Chet had taken, that first day home, on the motorcycle. His hand kept drifting down to touch the thick knot of bills in his pants pocket, fives and tens and twenties rolled together, and his eyes took in the splendor of the car he was driving.

He had stopped by a stream earlier and plastered the bright finish of the car with brown mud. And outside a tavern in Norton, he'd taken the plates off an Ohio car and substituted them for his.

Now, in his head, he was plunging forward, mapping his route. Pick up Jossie, up to Glade, take the Laurel Fork road south to Highway 250, then across the high pass and through the National Forest to Staunton. They would be out of West Virginia before morning, through Kentucky and well into Missouri by the next night, and the day after that they would be in Nebraska, taking their time, breathing the air, free and loose and clean. Starting over.

78

Jim August got out of his car, walked into the Elkins bus station, and up to the counter.

"You just made it," the ticket agent said. "That bus leaves in four minutes exact. Ten twenty-two."

In the loading lanes, Jim found the Chicago bus, half a dozen people waiting, the driver standing by the door.

"Anybody on the bus yet?" Jim asked him.

"Not yet. They'll board in a couple minutes."

"I'm looking for somebody who's on the run. You mind if I check it out first?"

"Help yourself."

Jim climbed the steps, moved slowly to the rear of the bus, opened the rest-room door, then walked back to the front and got off.

He stood beside the driver while the passengers handed over their tickets and boarded. He stayed there, watching, as the driver closed the door, tapped the horn twice, and pulled out of the station.

Jim went back inside the terminal, checked the coffee shop, the rest rooms, the baggage room, and every other corner of the building. Then he went outside and sat in his car, thinking and smoking. After three cigarettes he started his car, turned out of the station parking lot, and headed south again toward Kittredge, driving slowly now, his mind busy, only half-listening to the voice on his radio.

"The suspect was driving a 1976 Chrysler sedan, tan, four-door, last seen west of Elkins . . ."

Jim came alive. He turned up the volume on his radio.

". . . could be on eastbound Thirty-three or on Two Nineteen in the Huttonsville area. Repeat—this is the shotgun holdup suspect. Proceed with caution."

"I'll be a son-of-a-bitch," Jim said. "I'll be a *son-of-a-bitch.*" He jammed his foot down on the accelerator and the police car shot forward, motor throbbing, the light on the roof turning and flashing, burning red holes in the dark.

79

Jossie stayed at the window for more than an hour, trembling with anxiety and impatience and anticipation. Finally, when she couldn't sit still any longer, she got up, spread her suitcase open on the kitchen table, unpacked it slowly, refolded each piece of clothing, and put it back in place again in the bag.

She made fresh coffee, heated a pail of water, and mopped the kitchen floor. She washed off the table and the chairs, one by one, and polished the kitchen stove. And every few minutes, she broke the rhythm of her work by going to the window, pushing the curtain aside, and looking out.

At last, she took the family photograph album from the table in the parlor, carried it to the chair by the window in the kitchen and began to examine every picture on every page, slow and deliberate, spacing it out, making it last.

80

Kermit sat in his car in the woods till almost eleven o'clock, obeying some instinct he'd developed as a boy. Stalking, waiting, walking without a sound, no sound of breathing, even. A sense of timing, an unbending self-discipline, tools for matching himself against the fox, the grouse, the hare, whatever he was hunting. A quietness, inside and out, no ripples on the water, no wings in the air, no footfalls or heartbeats, a self-imposed and painless little death. Silence.

Then he got out of the car, closed the door, and stood in the spot where Jossie had met him with the motorcycle. The starting place. He untied the twine holding the burlap around the shotgun, folded the cloth into a pad, and polished the stock and the barrels with it. He tossed the burlap into the underbrush, cradled the shotgun on his arm, and walked away through the dark of the woods, heading for his house.

It was a twenty-minute walk. He'd made it many times in ten. He could have walked those paths with his eyes closed and his arms bound, trusting his feet and his senses, his animal memory.

But this night he moved deliberately, marking with his eyes each turn in the trail, each tree and gorge and hanging vine, each stump and fallen log, every spring and tangled ravine, every twist and turn, hollow and hummock.

Sighting stars through the trees, he moved like a warm shadow, feeling the night, full of it, seeing, smelling, and touching, tattooing it all on the front of his brain to remember and refer to. Tomorrow and the day after and all the time away, however long that might turn out to be.

81

When Kermit came to the house, he skirted the clearing, stayed in the woods, in the dark, till he came to a spot where he could see the kitchen window, a pale yellow square in the dark mass of the house. He stood there watching, filled with tomorrow and a warm sense of his God-given luck.

He stepped forward then, into the clearing, walked to

a spot forty feet from the window, whistled a bird call Jossie knew, and waited, sharply silhouetted in the silver light.

Inside the house, her ears tuned for any outside sound, Jossie heard the whistle. She ran from the parlor to the kitchen window, and pulled back the curtains.

Just then, from somewhere beside the house, a flashlight snapped on and a white circle of light focussed on Kermit's face. Jossie screamed, "Kermit . . ." but two gunshots, close together, drowned out her voice.

82

He was lying on his back in the grass when she got to him, crumpled and heavy, blood spreading across his chest and staining through his shirt.

She didn't speak and she didn't cry. She sank down to the ground and lifted his head into her lap, covering his face with her body, her arms around his shoulders, sealing in the warmth for as long as she could, allowing her skin to believe, to be deceived, to feel some last faint quiver of life.

She stayed there, absolutely still, seeing nothing, hearing nothing. Faintly conscious of footsteps, she didn't turn her head or raise her eyes.

At last, when Kermit's cheeks and his forehead and his hands were colder and smoother than anything else she remembered, she relaxed her arms and slowly lowered him to the ground.

Still on her knees, she raised her eyes, turned her head, and looked up at Jim August, twenty feet away to her left, standing like a totem, hatless, his arms at his sides, the revolver still in one hand, the flashlight in the other. Their eyes locked for an instant, then she looked down at Kermit again. She smoothed his hair back from his forehead, then sat quiet beside him, her hands folded together in her lap.

After a long moment, very deliberately, she reached across Kermit's body, picked up his shotgun, and turned it toward Jim.

They faced each other, silent, an endless frozen stillness. Then she squeezed the two triggers, felt the stock jolt against her shoulder, and watched his body hurtle backward, suspend in air like slow motion, then spread itself heavy and thick on the ground, half cut in two at the waist.

Slowly she put the gun down and cradled Kermit's head in her lap again.

Finally, she began to cry. And just then, for the first time, she felt movement, a flutter, a nudge of life inside her. She moved Kermit's head so his cool cheek was against her stomach. And she felt the movement again.